THE BIRDS

BY THE SAME AUTHOR

The Bridges
The House in the Dark
The Ice Palace
Spring Night

TARJEI VESAAS
THE BIRDS

Translated from the Norwegian by
TORBJØRN STØVERUD and MICHAEL BARNES

PETER OWEN
LONDON AND CHESTER SPRINGS

PETER OWEN LTD
73 Kenway Road, London SW5 0RE

Peter Owen books are distributed in the USA by
Dufour Editions Inc., Chester Springs, PA 19425-0007

Translated from the Norwegian *Fuglane*

This paperback edition 2002
English translation first published 1968
© Gyldendal Norsk Forlag A/S 1957
English translation © Peter Owen Ltd 1968, 1995

A catalogue record for this book is available from
the British Library

ISBN 0 7206 1143 1

Printed and bound in Great Britain by
Bookmarque Ltd, Croydon, Surrey

Part One

1

It was evening. Mattis looked to see if the sky was clear and free of cloud. It was. Then he said to his sister Hege, to cheer her up : 'You're like lightning.'

The word sent a cold shiver down his spine, but he felt safe all the same, seeing the sky was so perfect.

'With those knitting needles of yours, I mean,' he added.

Hege nodded unconcerned and went on with the large sweater she was making. Her knitting needles were flashing. She was working on an enormous eight-petalled rose which some man would soon be wearing.

'Yes, I know,' she said simply.

'But then I'm really grateful for all you do, Hege.'

He was slowly tapping his knee with his middle finger— the way he always did when he was thinking. Up and down, up and down. Hege had long since grown tired of asking him to give up this irritating habit.

Mattis went on : 'But you're not only like lightning with eight-petalled roses, it's the same with everything you do.'

She waved him aside : 'Yes, yes, I know.'

Mattis was satisfied and said no more.

It was using the word lightning he found so tempting. Strange lines seemed to form inside his head when he used it, and he felt himself drawn towards it. He was terrified of the lightning in the sky—and he never used the word in hot summer weather when there were heavy clouds. But tonight he was safe. They had had two storms already this spring, with real crashing thunder. As usual, when the storm was at its height Mattis had hidden himself in the privy; for someone had once told him that lightning had

7

never struck such buildings. Mattis wasn't sure whether this applied to the whole world, but where he was at least it had proved blissfully true so far.

'Yes, lightning,' he mumbled, half to himself, half to Hege, who was tired of this sudden bragging tonight. But Mattis hadn't finished.

'I mean at thinking, too,' he said.

At this she looked up quickly, as if frightened; something dangerous had been mentioned.

'That'll do for now,' she said and closed the matter abruptly.

'What's wrong?' he asked.

'Nothing. Just you sit quiet.'

Hege managed to suppress whatever was trying to come out. The fact was that the tragedy of her simple brother had haunted her for so long now that whenever Mattis used the word 'think' she jumped as if she'd been stung.

Mattis knew something was wrong, but he associated it with the bad conscience he always had because he didn't work like other people. He rattled off his set piece : 'You must find me some work tomorrow. Things can't go on like this.'

'Yes,' she said, not thinking.

'I can't allow this to go on. I haven't earned anything for—'

'No, it's a long time since you last came home with anything,' she blurted out, a little carelessly, a little sharply. She regretted it the moment it was said; Mattis was very sensitive to criticism on this point, unless he was doing the criticizing himself.

'You shouldn't say things like that to me,' he told her, and there was an odd expression on his face.

She blushed and bent her head. But Mattis went on : 'Why don't you talk to me as you would to anyone else?'

'Yes, all right.'

8

Hege kept her head down. Whatever could she do with things as they were? Sometimes she couldn't control herself and it was then her words hurt.

2

Brother and sister were sitting on the front steps outside the simple cottage where they lived by themselves. It was a fine, warm June evening, and the old woodwork gave off a lazy smell after a day of sunshine.

They had been sitting there for a long time without saying a word—until they began talking about lightning, and about earning money. Just sitting there, side by side. Mattis sat looking at the treetops with a steady gaze. This sitting of his was a familiar sight to his sister too. She knew he couldn't help it, or she'd no doubt have asked him to stop it.

The two of them lived here by themselves—there were no other houses—but there was a road and a large cluster of farms just beyond the line of spruces. In the other direction sparkles of light were coming from a broad lake, with distant shores beyond. The lake came right up to the slope below the cottage, and here Hege and Mattis kept their boat. The small clearing round the house was fenced in and belonged to them, but beyond the fence brother and sister had no say.

Mattis thought: She doesn't know what I'm looking at. He felt tempted to tell her.

Mattis and Hege—they've got doubles! Hege doesn't know that.

He didn't tell her.

Just beyond the fence stood two withered aspen trees,

9

their bare, white tops jutting up among the green spruces. They stood close to each other, and among people in the village they were called *Mattis-and-Hege*, though not openly. It was only by accident that Mattis had got to hear the names. They were almost contracted into one word: Mattis-and-Hege. They must have been in use a long time before Mattis heard them.

Two withered aspen trees side by side, in among the green growing spruces.

He felt a stirring of protest against the names and couldn't stop looking at the trees. But Hege must never get to know the secret, he decided, every time they sat there like this. She'll only fly into a rage and get angry—and the tree's got its name now anyway.

At the same time the very fact that the two trees remained there gave Mattis a quiet sense of protection. Admittedly they were nothing but a nuisance, and did damage where they stood, but the owner didn't come and cut them down in front of your very eyes and throw them on to his fire. That would have been too awful somehow, here, in front of the people who were smarting under the names—almost like murder. And that's why he doesn't do it. I should like to meet that man some day, thought Mattis. But then he never comes here.

Mattis went on thinking:

I wonder what he's like inside, the man who found such pleasure in inventing those names for the tree-tops? Impossible to say. All you could do was sit and think about it during summer evenings here on the steps. But it was a man who'd done it. Mattis refused to think it had been done by a woman; his feelings towards women were friendly. He was angry, too, that Hege had been compared to a withered tree-top, it was nothing like her! Surely anyone could see that. Hege, who was so clever and wise.

What is it that hurts so much?

You know very well, came the reply, somehow meaningless, yet straight to the point.

I ought to turn away and not look—instead I sit staring at them, first thing in the morning and last thing at night. Nothing could be crazier than that.

'Mattis?'

He was jerked out of his thoughts.

'What is it you can see?' she asked.

He knew these questions of hers so well. He mustn't sit like that, mustn't do this and mustn't do that, he ought to be like other people, not Simple Simon as they called him, the laughing stock wherever he went and tried to work or do anything else. Quickly he turned his eyes on his sister. Strange eyes. Always helpless, shy like birds.

'I can't see anyone,' he said.

'Oh.'

'You are strange,' he said. 'If I saw something every time I looked around—what would it be like here? The whole place would be crowded.'

Hege just nodded. She had somehow brought him back and could go on working. She never sat idle on the steps like Mattis, her hands were busy knitting, as they had to be.

Mattis looked at her work with respect, this was what kept their home going, going as best it could. He himself earned nothing. Nobody wanted him. They called him Simple Simon and laughed whenever his name was mentioned in connection with work. The two things just didn't go together. There were probably dozens of stories going round among their busy neighbours in the village about what happened when Simple Simon tried to work—everything always went wrong.

You my beak against rock he suddenly thought as he sat there—and gave a start.

What?

11

But it was gone.

The image and the words shot through him. And were gone again just as quickly—instead he seemed to be staring at a blank wall. He flung a quick glance at his sister but she hadn't noticed anything. She sat there small and neat, but no girl any more, she was forty years old.

Suppose he mentioned things like that to her? Beak against—she wouldn't understand.

Hege was sitting close to him, so he had a good view of her straight, dark brown hair. Suddenly he noticed a grey hair here and there among the brown ones. Long silvery threads.

Have I the eyes of a hawk today? he thought in a flash of happy wonder, I've never noticed this before. Impulsively he exclaimed: 'But Hege!'

She looked up quickly, reassured by the tone of his voice. Ready to join in: 'What is it?'

'You're starting to go grey!'

She bent her head.

'Am I?'

'Very grey,' he said. 'I never noticed it until today. Did you know about it?'

There was no reply.

'It's jolly early,' he said. 'After all, you're only forty, and so grey.'

Suddenly he felt somebody looking at him from somewhere. Not Hege. From somewhere. A cutting glance. Perhaps it was coming from Hege after all. He felt frightened and realized he had done something wrong, yet without really being aware of it; after all he had only been observant.

'Hege.'

At last she looked up.

'What's the matter now, then?'

No, what he wanted to say had gone. No more glances either.

'It's nothing really,' he said. 'Just get on with your knitting.'

She smiled and said : 'All right then, Mattis.'

'Yes, and you don't mind, do you?' he asked gently. 'My talking about your grey hairs?'

She just tossed her hair as if in a kind of half-merry obstinacy : 'Not really. I knew about it already, you see.'

Her flashing knitting needles had been busy the whole time. They seemed to work automatically all day long.

'Yes, you're sharp-witted, you really are,' he said, to make up for what he shouldn't have said.

This gave him another opportunity to use one of those words that hung before him, shining and alluring. Far away in the distance there were more of them, dangerously sharp. Words that were not for him, but which he used all the same on the sly, and which had an exciting flavour and gave him a tingling feeling in the head. They were a little dangerous, all of them.

'Do you hear, Hege?'

She sighed : 'Yes.'

Nothing more. Oh well, that was how she was. Perhaps he praised her too much?

But really, that's too early to be going grey, he mumbled softly so she didn't hear it. What about me, I wonder? I must have a look before I forget.

'Are you going to bed, Mattis?'

'No, I'm only—' going to take a look in the mirror, he nearly blurted out, but stopped himself and went indoors.

3

It was only as Mattis entered the house that he noticed what a lovely evening it was. The big lake was as calm as a mill-pond. Beyond it, the ridges to the west were covered in haze—they usually were. There was a smell of early summer. On the road, which was hidden behind the trees, the cars seemed to be humming just for the fun of it. The sky was clear, there would be no thunder during the night.

Straight through lightning, he thought, and shuddered.

Straight through straight, he thought.

If only one could.

He remained standing deep in thought by the bench that opened up and became his bed at night.

From an early age Mattis had slept in the bench in the sitting-room—so he really knew it well. He'd decided he'd go on doing it for the rest of his life. There were scratches in the bench from the time when Mattis was a boy and had been given a knife. There were also thick, faded pencil marks on the unpainted wood, from the time when he had been given a pencil. These lines and strange figures lay underneath the lid, and he looked at them every night before he went to sleep, and liked them because they never changed. They were what they were supposed to be. You could rely on them.

The little room at the back was Hege's. Mattis tore himself away and went into it, for that was where the only mirror in the house hung.

He entered her room. There was a clean smell there, but little else, apart from the mirror he needed.

14

'Hm!' he exclaimed as he caught sight of himself in the glass.

It really was a long time since he had looked at himself in the mirror in this way. Now and then he came in here to fetch the mirror when he was going to shave. But then he concentrated on shaving, and even so he didn't get the stubble off properly.

Now he was looking at Mattis, sort of.

Oh gosh! said a voice inside him. A silent little cry he couldn't really explain.

'Not much to look at,' he mumbled.

'Not much fat,' he added.

'Not much flesh either.'

'Badly shaven,' he said.

It sounded depressing.

'But there's something though,' he said quickly and went on looking.

The mirror was not particularly good either, it distorted the image—but both he and Hege had got used to this over the years.

Mattis hadn't been in there long before his thoughts began to wander, standing as he was in this clean-smelling, feminine room.

I'm standing looking at myself in the mirror like a girl, he thought, and felt a sense of well-being creeping over him.

I'm sure many a girl has stood looking at herself in the worn glass of this mirror before putting on her clothes.

He conjured up many beautiful, alluring pictures.

Let me think of *them*.

But he stopped himself.

No, mustn't think of girls in the middle of the week. That's not allowed. Nobody does that.

He felt uncertain: I'm afraid I do, now and then, he admitted.

But nobody knows.

He looked himself in the face. Caught his glance. It was immediately filled with defiance. Surely I can, as long as I don't tell anybody.

It's just the way I am.

He caught his glance again. His eyes widened and opened out, full of expectation.

What's this?

Well I never, said a voice inside him, full of wonder, yet addressed to no one in particular. Sometimes you had to say things like this, almost for no reason, for far less reason than he had now.

'But this *isn't* much to look at,' he said aloud. He had to brush aside all the things which had taken possession of him, but which didn't belong to the moment.

The face opposite him was thin and full of thought. Pale, but a pair of eyes pulled at him and wouldn't let go.

He felt like saying to the person in front of him : Where on earth do you come from !

Why did you come?

There would be no reply.

But it was to be found in those eyes—eyes which were not his, but came from far off and had looked through night and day. It came nearer, it lit up. Then it was gone again and all was black.

He thought quickly : Mattis the Simpleton.

Simple Simon.

How they'd have laughed if they'd seen me standing here, looking at myself in the mirror.

At last he remembered what he'd really come into Hege's room for. He'd come to look for grey hairs.

None in front. He bent his head, and in his search for grey hairs on top his eyes rolled upwards under the lock of hair that fell over his forehead. Not a single one. Afterwards he peered as far back behind each ear as he could. Not a single grey hair anywhere. And he was only three years younger than Hege after all, and she was forty.

No, here's a fellow with hair that'll last him for some time, he thought.

But in three years I'll have caught up with Hege.

Not a single grey hair. My word, I'm going to tell Hege about this and give her a real fright, he thought, forgetting that she hadn't liked this topic of conversation.

He strode out again. Hege was bound to be sitting on the steps with her knitting still.

There she was right enough. The sweater seemed to grow of its own accord in her quick hands. They were performing a kind of silent dance, while the sweater took shape, unaided.

'Well?' she said, seeing him come out in such a hurry.

Mattis pointed to his mop of hair :

'Not a single grey hair on me, Hege. I've been inside and looked in the mirror.'

Hege didn't want to discuss the subject again.

'I see,' she said curtly.

'Isn't it splendid?' he asked.

'Of course it's splendid,' she replied calmly.

'Yes, just look at you,' he said, 'I bet you wish—'

She couldn't control herself :

'Oh, for God's sake !'

He stopped at once. There was something about Hege that pulled him up short.

'Anything wrong?' he asked, frightened.

At last she got up.

'Mattis.'

He looked at her, nervously.

'Well, go on.'

'I don't think it's much fun, the way you're going on and on about this tonight.'

'Fun? What fun do you or I have?' he replied. What an odd thing for her to say, he thought.

Hege looked at him, helplessly, frightened all of a sudden. Something had to be done quickly, for Mattis was on the point of starting something she couldn't cope with.

'We have more fun than you realize,' she said firmly, driving the point home like a nail. 'It's just that you don't give it a thought. We have fun every single day.'

He bent his head, but asked : 'When?'

'When?' she said, sternly.

She went on again. This had to be stopped.

'Use your brains, Mattis,' she said, forgetting the usual sting. Stood above him, insistent, although she was the smaller.

Mattis replied : 'I'm thinking so hard it's almost killing me.'

'Then surely you remember heaps of fun.'

He thought, gave no reply.

Hege persisted. The fact had to be established so firmly that there was no room left for the slightest doubt.

'We have *more* fun than other people.'

'Do we really?' He started mumbling feebly, almost inaudibly.

'Yes !' she said. 'And you must never forget it.'

She left it at that. Mattis straightened up a little, but dared not protest. Hege was clever and no doubt knew what things were fun. Best not to protest and make a fool of oneself.

She looked at him angrily.

'I didn't realize this,' was all he said.

Then a bright idea suddenly struck him, and he said in a happy voice : 'It was a good thing you told me.'

'What?'

'Seeing I didn't know.'

He felt happy, laughed a little.

'Are you going in already?' he said.

Hege gave him a weary nod instead of answering, and went into the house.

4

Hege went to bed earlier than usual that evening, too. At least she went into her room earlier. Mattis was about to ask why, but before he managed to do so she stopped him with an impatient: 'Oh wait until tomorrow, Mattis! Please don't go on any more today.'

Listening to her, he lost the desire to ask any more questions. She was in a bad mood, she could go. He wondered if he'd done anything wrong. This business of her hair, no doubt. Was it so dreadful that her hair was grey while his wasn't? After all, he couldn't help it.

But it was Hege who kept him, so she had him well in her grip. Above all she was clever, and that was what he respected most.

Hege left him without saying another word. He stayed behind thinking about it all.

Tomorrow I must take a trip round the farms and see if anybody's got any work for me, he thought, dreading it already.

Because that's the root of the trouble. Hege keeps me all the year round. And so she has for forty years, he felt he might as well add. At least he wouldn't be making it out to be less than it actually was.

Keeps me. Keeps me.

The word had a bitter taste. It was like chewing the bark of an aspen tree. And chew it he had to, year in, year out. Sitting alone as he was now. He had to put it on his tongue and taste it. There was no escape. It was the bitterest of all the words he knew.

Tomorrow I'm going to work.

Provided nothing stops me, he added quickly, to be on the safe side. He had a hazy recollection of the many days when he'd started working for somebody. On a farm or in the fields, or in the forests. There was always something which upset things for him so that he couldn't finish the job. And after that they didn't ask him to work there any more. The clever ones, those who owned things and had jobs to offer, they passed him by without noticing him. And so he had to return to Hege with empty hands. She was so used to it now that she just accepted it. But she went on struggling in order to keep him. Wonder what she really *thought* about it all.

Be tough tomorrow. Face it bravely, go over to the farms and ask for a job.

'It can't go on like this for ever,' he said in a fierce tone into the empty air. 'I *must* get some work, Hege's gone grey.'

He began to realize : It's me who's made Hege go grey.

Gradually the whole truth of the matter dawned on him. He felt terribly ashamed of himself.

5

It grew late, much later than Mattis generally stayed up. All the same he didn't feel like going to bed, and went on strolling about outside. When you had something on your mind it was even worse lying in bed, twisting and turning.

Perhaps Hege isn't asleep either. She went into her room early just to avoid me.

'And it's not much fun knowing *that*,' he said in a loud voice, so loud that she could possibly have heard it in her room.

He felt very depressed.

A sudden thought made him start: You mustn't leave me! he gasped, turned towards the room where Hege lay. Whatever happens to you or me you mustn't leave me.

This was by no means a new thought, but it felt new each time, and just as painful. And each time he had to dismiss it as nonsense. Hege had never as much as breathed a word about leaving him. Why should he torment himself like this?

The vision would not leave him. He saw Hege walking away, farther and farther. She was carrying all her belongings in a little parcel under her arm.

Are you leaving?

Yes, Mattis.

Very sad this, Hege.

Yes, Mattis.

Then she began walking again.

She wasn't listening to him any more, she grew smaller and smaller, in the end she was only a tiny black dot—and there she remained. Couldn't disappear altogether in this sad charade.

Just at this moment came the great event.

He was deep in thought, having visions of Hege walking away, sitting in his usual place on the steps looking across the lake to the hills in the west. The lake was black now, and the hills deep and dark. A fine summer twilight everywhere, in the sky and on earth. Mattis was by no means blind to things like that.

Their cottage stood in a marshy little hollow which rose from the lake. Birches and aspens were dotted among the conifers. A little brook ran down through the hollow. Sometimes Mattis thought it was more beautiful here than any other place he had seen—of the few places he knew.

Perhaps this was what he felt now, too—he was certainly lost in contemplation and let the twilight grow deeper and deeper, in so far as you could call it twilight and not just something unspeakably gentle.

At that moment the unexpected happened.

This side of the wind it is still, he had just been thinking, as he stared towards the two aspens and the evening sky. Something was filtering through the tree-tops, it was so clear he felt he could see it. No wind, just something filtering through—and on this side it was so still that not a leaf on the other aspens trembled.

But then came a tiny little sound: all of a sudden a strange cry, and at the same time he could just make out quick flapping wings in the air above him. Then came more faint calls in a helpless bird language.

It went straight across the house.

But it went straight through Mattis as well. A wordless excitement arose inside him; he sat there wide awake and confused.

Was it magic?

No, anything but, and yet—

It was a woodcock that had flapped over the house, and the woodcock didn't do that sort of thing by chance, not at this time of day. A flight had begun over his house!

When had it started?

Because it hadn't been there any spring before, as far back as he could remember. He'd been out late enough to have seen and heard it if it had.

But tonight it was going right overhead, over Hege and himself, and that's how it would be from now on, every single morning and evening.

Mattis looked at his house. It seemed to be a different house now, you had to look at it with different eyes. The

22

woodcock had always seemed to be something that glided through valleys far away from all that was his. That was how he had always imagined it. Now, this evening, it was here, it had simply moved right here. That's to say if it wasn't an illusion—he knew he was given to illusions. Had anyone ever heard of a woodcock moving from its usual path? Not as far as he knew. And why had it come here?

Mattis sat waiting almost breathless. For if it was a proper flight, the bird would return in a little while, along the same path, again and again during the short hour that the evening flight lasted. He knew this from other areas where flights occurred. Early in the morning, too, the bird moved along the same path, a fowler had told him so. On dry marshland he had sometimes seen the marks of woodcocks' beaks, next to the imprints of their dainty feet.

He sat waiting, full of excitement. The moments seemed to drag on, and his doubts grew stronger.

But hush, there it was. The flapping wings, the bird itself, indistinct, speeding through the air straight across the house and off in the other direction. Gone again, hidden by the gentle dusk and the sleeping tree-tops.

Then Mattis said in a firm voice : 'So the woodcock came at last.'

He didn't know how or why he said this. It was the least he could say and do—and no one was listening as he said it. He felt as if something were over and done with, after a long and difficult time.

His first thought was to tell Hege about it, he wanted to rush in right away. Sleeping or awake, she must hear about this at once. But he stopped. *If* it was true, then the bird would soon be back for a third time, and Mattis was so unsure of himself that he felt he had to wait for this third appearance. Sit and wait full of joy.

Hege's *got to* believe me if I've seen it three times. Everybody'll have to believe it then.

Hush, there it was again.

Just as before, the flapping, the shadow in the dusk, quick as an arrow—and then the faint call, whether anyone was listening or not. Straight across the roof, and away, out into space. Then it was simply late evening once more.

But it's come. Now I know something, he concluded, without going any further into the matter. There was no doubt about it, he felt different.

And Hege asleep.

Now Hege would be able to feel different too.

6

Hege asleep—Hege who was like lightning with her eight-petalled roses and sweaters, and who could cope with difficulties—Mattis was no longer sure which of them was more important. At this moment he almost felt like putting himself first.

He went into her room, making quite a noise.

It was a silly thing to do. Hege had long since gone to bed, perhaps even fallen asleep, so this was an unfortunate moment to disturb her. Her tone was rather sharp.

'What's the matter now?' she burst out before he could find words for his overflowing emotions. He recognized this tone only too well. She had obviously just fallen asleep, and then he came tramping in. But he also knew what would follow; she was already clearing her throat as a way of softening the impact of her first wounding remark.

'What is it, Mattis?' she said wearily, in a low voice that was now friendly and full of remorse.

The news Mattis was bringing was great. He hardly

knew how to put it into words. In the end he said simply:
'There's a woodcock started flying over here tonight!' His
voice was hard and inflexible. He almost felt like a stranger
standing by her bed.

Hege seemed to notice the tone of his voice. A tongue
numbed by wonder and awe. But there'd been so many
strange things that Mattis had come rushing to tell her.
Things that were usually soon explained and no longer
strange. She said quietly:

'A woodcock? Oh, I see. Well, go and get some sleep
now, Mattis.'

He didn't understand.

'Go to bed now, Mattis,' she said gently, seeing the dis-
traught expression on his face.

Mattis groaned with disappointment.

'Didn't you hear what I said? There's a woodcock here!
It's moved! It's flying straight across the roof of our
house! Now! This very minute, while you're sitting there
in bed.'

Hege remained sitting as before, with the same expression on her face.

'Of course I heard. But what of it? Can't you let the
woodcock come and go as it likes?'

He didn't understand her. It was as if she were speaking
a language he didn't understand.

'Doesn't it mean anything to you? Have you ever heard
of a woodcock changing its path like that and going right
over your head?'

She shrugged her shoulders.

'What's the good of asking me?'

'No, I bet you haven't. Put on your things now and
come outside.'

'Outside? Now, in the middle of the night?'

'Of course! You must see it too.'

'No, Mattis,' she said.

'You must! It's going on out there now. If this isn't anything important either, then—'

Hege's only reply was to lie down again. She yawned, heavy with sleep.

'I'm sure you found it fun to watch,' she said, 'but surely I can see it some other time. If it's here, it's here, isn't it?'

Mattis stared at her open-mouthed.

'If it's here, it's here!' he repeated horrified. 'And you're supposed to be clever?' he blurted out without thinking.

'What do you mean?' she asked.

'You don't understand anything then,' he summed up.

He stood over her, disappointed and helpless.

Gently she touched his arm. He took it as a sign of friendship. He didn't see how worn out and miserable Hege was at this moment. She lay there in her faded night-dress, not looking at him, her face turned to the wall.

'Let's talk about this in the morning, Mattis. Go to bed now, do you hear?'

To Mattis it sounded like madness—throwing away a chance like this.

'I'm telling you it's going on *now*. And you don't want to come out and see? I can't understand you. Nothing seems to mean anything to you.'

Finally Hege couldn't stand it any longer. She beat her hand against the edge of her bed and cried: 'You don't know what you're talking about. And coming from *you*, you who are—' She stopped suddenly.

He asked in a frightened voice: 'What am I?'

With her back to him, she shouted: 'Leave me in peace, please! I can't go on any longer if you don't— Oh, please go away, it's very late and we must get some sleep, Mattis.'

She gave a jerk, turning even farther away from him. He saw her shoulders begin to quiver. It shook him profoundly, made him feel guilty, whether he was or not.

He felt bewildered. Had he been unkind to her? He'd simply wanted to please her with the woodcock. It didn't occur to him that it wasn't as great an event for Hege as it was for him. It was going on out there now, this very minute—and Hege didn't care, shouted at him, and lay there weeping in incomprehensible helplessness.

'But Hege—I meant no harm, I just wanted you to—'

But now she was absolutely wild: 'Did you hear what I said,' she screamed, and he hastily retreated the few steps that were necessary to get out of her room. He closed the door gently, as if Hege were asleep and mustn't be disturbed.

How different people are, he thought in a bewildered way when he got outside. At least, Hege and I are. I don't think she even believes me. But I saw it and I heard it. I'll swear I saw it. The flight's just finished for tonight, that's all.

And now let's sing a song, said a voice inside him. Not that he began singing. It just seemed to follow on naturally after 'finished for tonight'. I've been to all sorts of meetings, so I've got a pretty good idea of how things are done there.

Finished for tonight. For now the bird has found his true-love.

When he looked up, there were beams of light where the woodcock had flown. Straight over his house.

To be quite honest he wasn't absolutely sure about this— but he felt that something had happened up there, that a change had taken place. And tomorrow it will all happen again, as wonderful as it was tonight. And Hege's going to see it, even if I have to tie her up out here.

Things are going to be different from now on, he thought before falling asleep, curled up in his bench like a child.

For me?

27

The thought sent a flood of warmth through him.

7

The woodcock followed Mattis into his sleep, and whoever he had to thank for it, a wonderful dream followed.

First of all a good omen, before anything actually appeared :

'We're coming, we're coming,' somebody said. 'You're ready, aren't you?'

'Yes, of course,' he was able to reply.

'It's taken a long time, Mattis,' said a friendly voice, 'but that's all over now.'

And it did indeed come. A bright beam above the house and on both sides, high and low, and a sound that was only just audible—as sounds like that ought to be. Immediately the house changed and became completely new.

'But it isn't the house that's the most important thing,' he said.

No, and it wasn't the other things either, it was he himself. The beams had gone right through him and made him quite different. When he bent his right arm to test his new muscles, there was such a bulge that the whole of the upper part of his shirt sleeve burst open. He looked at the smooth, beautifully-shaped muscle and laughed.

'That's better,' he said.

'That's really something to squeeze with,' he said with a sharp glance around him.

'Where are you?' he shouted.

They laughed, hidden in the grove.

'We're where we usually are.'

His house was really new and he went over to look at his reflection in the window panes. He'd never seen such a tough fellow as the one who faced him in the dark glass. He could see himself from every angle, and it all looked equally good.

He shouted proudly: 'Can you see anything?'

'Yes you bet we can,' came the reply from the grove. 'We can't see anything else.'

'Wait a bit,' he said, but a whole chorus replied: 'Wait? Now?'

'What are you going to do, Mattis?'

'Get ready, Mattis!'

'Yes, you bet I will,' he said, using their own expression.

He shook his head and no sooner had he done so than it was full of all the right words to say to girls—and to other people, too, for that matter. Not just helpless flickers as before. He laughed and played about with this new gift, trying out one or two of the bold words.

'Hey! You in the grove,' he said. 'Are you ready?'

'We're ready,' they said. 'Who do you want to come?'

'Will you come? You, the one I'm thinking of,' he said, letting his shirt tighten round his arm.

It was a tense moment, but the reply came at once: 'That's what I'd like to do.'

The other voices seemed to have sunk into the ground.

There she was, standing in front of her grove, no longer hidden. He had seen her in his imagination a thousand times, but still she was different. All the same he recognized her somehow and he wasn't a bit frightened. She came right up to him, surrounded by a gentle fragrance.

He mustn't touch her yet.

'Do something,' he said.

She understood at once.

'Yes,' she said, 'look.'

29

She waved her arm, and all around the air was filled with the song of birds.

'Yes, and you were born in the flight of the woodcock,' Mattis began, 'and you've long been in my thoughts. If there's something you want to say, you must say it now.'

'Say?' she said.

'Yes.'

'No, there's nothing more I want to say now.'

He looked straight into her eyes. At the same time he quietly bent his left arm, making his shirt sleeve tear with a little rip. The enormous, smooth, round muscles glistened in the sun right in front of her face.

'Nothing to worry about,' he said calmly. 'I've got plenty of shirts.'

'And the *left* arm!' she said, full of amazement.

'Yes,' he said, dismissing the matter, 'the right sleeve got torn long ago.'

She said no more, was so fascinated by what she saw that words failed her. That was how he had wished it. All his wishes were coming true. And what was more he was able to say things in the right way.

'Now you do just what you want,' he said to her. 'You're wonderful.'

She came nearer at once.

'I'm beginning to understand better now why I've been waiting so long,' he added.

She remained silent the whole time—because she had a secret she wanted to tell him. All she did was to come closer. She had waved her arm and all around the air had been filled with the song of birds—now she moved her whole body and he was spellbound by her magic.

Moved her whole body, and he couldn't say what happened. Something nameless. She was coming nearer, that was all. She was close to him, born of the flight of a woodcock, she belonged to him.

8

As usual Hege was the first to get up. Mattis was wide awake, but stayed in bed re-living his dream. He heard Hege moving about in her room. Then she came out. Mattis hurriedly turned towards the wall and pretended to be asleep. That seemed the safest thing to do, after the way they'd parted last night.

Hege stopped by him for a moment on her way out to the kitchen. Tense. But it passed. She moved on again. Soon he heard the familiar morning sounds of cups and knives.

Things are going to be different, Mattis thought dreamily. He found his clothes and got dressed. Felt different already, seemed to be supported by two strong arms—the woodcock and the dream, one on each side. He couldn't help listening to see if anything special was going to happen today as well. An unexpected word or some pleasant surprise might be waiting for him—now that things were different.

Not yet. But today mustn't be like any other day. He'd have to make sure of that himself.

'Early bird,' he said to Hege from the kitchen door. Part of the old proverb came to him, and he used it instead of saying good morning.

He felt unsure of himself. His last glimpse of Hege the night before had been unbearably sad. He could only think it was his fault she'd been lying there turned to the wall, crying.

And just afterwards *he* had the dream!

At any rate, Hege had got over it now after her night's

31

sleep. She stood there, small and agile, cutting bread. It almost looked as if she were making a special point of being carefree and unruffled, to smooth things over after last night. She answered his words about the early bird: 'You're in a good mood, aren't you?'

He laughed inwardly, but replied: 'How do you mean?'

'Well, aren't you?'

'You don't know why,' he said.

Not a word from her about last night. And then she almost went too far: 'I think I do. It's because you're off to do something really big today, just as we said. And I'm sure the early bird'll come home with the worm.'

Oh no! He'd forgotten he'd promised to go and look for work. But Hege hadn't forgotten, that was pretty obvious. There was no denying this cast a shadow over his joy.

'No, you're wrong there,' he said.

'But aren't you—'

'There's a woodcock here now,' he interrupted her. He said it as one offering information, to explain the new state of affairs. Surely he wasn't expected to make the painful trip round the farms asking for work now, when so many pleasant things had happened.

But Hege wasn't the least bit moved.

'So what?' she said. 'What difference does it make whether there's a woodcock here or not?'

'I don't really know. Are you sure *you* don't know either?' He felt braver now, but it was no use.

'Eat your breakfast,' said Hege.

And so he did. He was still living in his dream. He would have to make Hege understand later, understand the important thing that had happened, and which she refused to accept.

All of a sudden he broke the silence: 'Hm!' he said and tapped the floor three times with the toe of his shoe.

'Well?'

'Nothing to do with *you*.'

'Isn't it?' said Hege. 'You look as if you're bursting to say something.'

Mattis ate several mouthfuls without saying anything, but he couldn't restrain himself.

'It's strange the kind of things people can dream, if they really want to,' he said.

Hege wasn't playing along with him.

'Oh, so you've been dreaming,' she said, as if the whole thing was of no importance at all.

'Hm!' said Mattis once more.

'You'd better tell me, or you'll burst.'

Her reaction made the dream still more vivid and real. It seemed almost true.

'Tell you what I dreamt?'

She nodded.

'I can't,' he said earnestly and looked at her with wide open eyes.

'Then it can't have been much of a dream,' Hege said a little snappily, pouring him some of the weak coffee they always drank. She was already starting to move away from him.

Mattis said: 'Decent people don't talk about the kind of thing I dreamt about. So now you know.'

'Oh?'

'It's no good your asking and asking. Now you can guess, surely.'

She didn't grow the least bit more curious, poured cold water on the whole thing: 'Well, you can console yourself with the fact that dreams always go by opposites. The reverse of what you dream comes true.'

'What!' he burst out. Her words made him shudder. It sounded as if she wanted to hurt him. But she didn't know what she was talking about, that's what it was. 'That was a nastier thing to say than you know,' he said horrified,

33

and refused to eat any more. He got up so abruptly that he took the top of the table with him—sitting squeezed in as he was. The weak coffee ran all over the place and a cup smashed as well.

'What a mess you're making, Mattis.'

'Well, who's fault is that?'

Surely she understood how she was spoiling everything for him.

'But I won't allow you to spoil it for me,' he said.

'Calm down now, Mattis.'

He pulled himself together :

'No, it doesn't matter, because things are going to be different from now on. It began last night.'

Hege remembered how cross she had been the night before and felt sorry about it.

'I *will* come with you and look at that woodcock one evening. Only don't keep on about it.'

'It'll never be like the first time.'

Hege left it at that, cleared the table, and took the half-finished sweater. Meanwhile she kept an eye on Mattis to see what he was going to do. He could feel her looking at him and asked in an irritated voice : 'What's the matter now, then?'

'I'm waiting to see whether you're going over to the farms, as you said you would.'

She had no mercy.

'But the woodcock—'

Hege hardened.

'Woodcock, birds, that's no excuse. You said you were going, and now you must go.'

Mattis became frightened. Hege must really have set her mind on it this time, seeing she was so stubborn. Did she still not understand what misery this caused him? He got up from the security of his chair and asked uneasily : 'Is this how things are different here after the woodcock?'

34

'We must never give in,' said Hege, 'I've told you so a thousand times.'

'It's easy for you to talk.'

He pondered for a while.

'Why don't I have muscles big enough to rip my shirt?' he said, and his voice was loud and harsh.

Hege made no reply.

'You never ask me!' he went on in his excitement.

'What about?'

'The sort of things people *don't* ask about.'

Hege's voice was sharp: 'Stop it now.'

They had touched on matters that were awkward for both of them.

'Can I wait till tomorrow?' he asked, referring to the humiliating trip round the farms to look for work. She had so often been a good sister to him—but now she was beginning to lose her temper more easily than before.

'Today is *today*, you see.'

'All right, we'll call that a bargain,' said Hege.

9

Today was today.

Mattis went strolling around.

There were three things in the dream, he thought to himself.

I was different in three different ways.

He was walking about in the warmth of a fine summer morning. Hege was probably sitting indoors sulking because he refused to go and look for work. Well, he couldn't help that. Recent events were too near and too important. Sweet smells and fresh breezes were all around him.

Three great changes. They were gone again this morning, there was no doubt about that. He had nothing but the memory of it all, quivering beneath him like the strings of a fiddle. It was as though he happened to tread on one of these strings on the ground below, and a sound rang out, magical, real and true.

Different in three different ways—but today was today. Strange how little Hege seems to understand, he thought, and went down to the lake.

There he stood throwing stones into the water like a child. The lake was absolutely smooth, there was no point at all in trying to fish, so he could safely leave his ramshackle old boat where it was.

The three things. They were around him somewhere, and last night he and they had been one. All the things in himself that he wished were different had been different.

He stood there tossing stones into the lake with a glazed and far-away expression in his eyes, heavy stones that fell with a splash.

'Mattis! Lunch!' Hege called down to him from the cottage. The comforting sound of a woman about the house.

The three things gave a jump.

There was no need for her to shout 'come at once!' Mattis was quick enough when he was called to a meal. He hurried up the slope and sat down at the table.

'You'd better eat while you can,' said Hege, pushing the plate across to him. He knew very well that her tone had something to do with his refusal to go out and look for work. That was why she was talking to him like this.

'If only one was different in three ways,' he said as he ate.

'What three ways?'

'It's to do with what I didn't tell you. And with girls and—'

36

'All right, but finish your food.'

'You're always the same,' he said in a peevish voice. 'You just can't understand.'

'Yes,' said Hege, 'but are you going to make that trip tomorrow?'

How strange and stubborn she is, he thought, but then that's the way you get food.

'If I've said I'll do it then I'll do it,' he replied, shuddering at the thought of standing helpless, exposed to the gaze of really efficient workers.

Hege was busy with the sweater she was making. Mattis said almost entreatingly : 'Are you going to watch the bird when it comes back this evening? This morning you said you would some time.'

'Not this evening, it means being up so late.'

'But you said—'

'I'd rather get some sleep,' said Hege firmly.

'But supposing you never woke up again!' said Mattis harshly. 'You'd be really sorry then.'

She gave a start. His words had an effect he didn't understand.

'Stop it, Mattis,' she shouted.

He fled. He heard her saying something behind him, but he slunk out of the door, frightened.

That evening he sat on the steps, uneasy, fidgeting nervously with his fingers. Hege had taken the risk and gone to bed after all.

The time came for the bird to appear.

There was his cry, and there came the wings, flapping helplessly somehow, beating quickly.

The wings were high up in the mild night air, but at the same time they touched the very centre of Mattis's heart. The soft, dark touch of something beyond understanding.

37

It spread right through him. Me and the woodcock, sort of, ran his formless train of thought.

In his joy he made a promise : tomorrow I'll go just as Hege wants, as long as there isn't a thunderstorm. Lightning is lightning. I shan't go then—and well she knows it.

He waited for the woodcock to fly across twice more before going to bed in a room filled with the warmth and half-light of a summer's night. But if he had expected the *dream* to reappear, he was disappointed. There was not so much as a hint of a grove full of girls.

10

The two aspens, Mattis-and-Hege, stood pointing up into the morning sun and the deep blue sky. Mattis walked past them and up on to the road. He was walking with his lips pressed tightly together. What's the woodcock come for if everything's going to stay the same as before? Wouldn't the best thing be just to wait and see if anything happened? No, Hege had said.

He wasn't quite so eager now as the night before after he'd been greeted by the bird.

If Hege had been a different sort of person she'd never have sent him out on this pointless trip, she'd have realized she shouldn't. But Hege'll never be different. Doesn't need to be either, somehow.

He plodded on.

As soon as he came out of the wood a whole cluster of farms lay stretched out before him. Almost every one of them held the memory of an unsuccessful attempt to work.

The road was busy already. As usual the cars were forcing people into the side. The verges were grey with dust that had been thrown up into the air.

Mattis sometimes walked along this road even if he wasn't looking for work. Occasionally Hege sent him to the store with a little money to buy food, or with a sweater she'd finished. It was always a risky business, it might turn out well, but it could also end in shame and disgrace.

Round about on the farms people were just starting work for the day. Mattis saw them all around him. The first jobs of summer, mostly weeding. They looked sturdy and able, set off for work as though it were just as natural a thing as living and breathing. Some were puffing away at a morning pipe, others were using their mouths to whistle, and some were just swinging their arms.

Should he go and ask straight away? Go into the nearest farmyard? No, better not. They'd only feel embarrassed because they had to invent some excuse about its not being convenient today. He left one farm after another undisturbed. He imagined people sighing with relief as he walked past and they saw his back disappearing.

But *they* can't have had a dream like the one I've had! he thought, and this cheered him up.

He could remember lots of embarrassing episodes, some worse than others. A number of the men he passed on the road were people he'd tried to work with, and the memory of it made him fix his eyes on the ground. Those he met mostly hurried past as well—as if their last encounter were something they both wanted to forget.

It's bound to be the same today. Hege knows it very well, and so do I. I'll turn round and go back now, he thought. I can't go into these farms where everybody knows me already.

But strangely, no sooner had the thought occurred to him than he did exactly the opposite. He left the main road and strode up into a farmyard. What had come over him? A memory had flashed into his mind. He remembered a little episode which hadn't ended in disgrace, one that had taken place in that very farmyard.

Maybe he'd find something there to bolster him up today, too.

Mattis met the farmer just by the corner of the house. He was standing there with a young man and a girl, and they were each holding a light hoe, ready to set off for the turnip field. Mattis didn't look at them until he was very close, then suddenly his face appeared in front of them as if out of nowhere.

'Good morning—any chance of a job here?' he asked hurriedly, and his anxious eyes looked searchingly at the farmer. He must avoid giving himself time for second thoughts. He managed to edge his way round so that he got the two young people behind him.

To his surprise the farmer's answer came straight away; he hadn't had time for second thoughts either.

'Yes, if you can thin out turnips.'

Mattis gaped a little, then he smiled broadly.

'Just as I thought,' he said. 'If things are different from before, this is how they must be.'

'What do you mean?'

'Oh just something,' said Mattis. 'Something that's very different for me today. But it's something you don't know anything about.'

The girl and the young man had moved so that they were now in front of Mattis. They began exchanging glances in a way that Mattis knew only too well, and which didn't bode well for him.

'It's to do with the flight of a woodcock,' Mattis said quickly and nervously to the farmer.

'The flight of a woodcock?'

'Yes, don't you know what that is?' Mattis asked, feeling better.

The farmer no doubt remembered by now who it was in front of him, but it was too late, he surely wouldn't go back on his word.

'I've heard of woodcocks,' he said. 'But it was this turnip field you wanted to have a go at, wasn't it? We'd better find a hoe for you too—then we can see who's the quickest at thinning out.'

The farmer felt he had to add this last remark, probably couldn't stop it coming out.

Mattis was sensitive, and he felt the impact.

'Yes, perhaps we could see who can run fastest too,' he said with a little laugh. He almost managed to make it sound like real laughter.

The farmer was a little surprised, but hurriedly joined in the laughter.

'You mean see who can get to the turnips first?'

They were both laughing, each trying to outdo the other.

'But I expect you'd like a bite to eat before you begin?' the farmer asked, putting an end to the fun.

Mattis shook his head.

'We've got plenty of food at home, thanks.'

Nice to be able to say things like that, he felt.

Now it was time to work. Mattis was given a hoe, and they all walked across to the turnip field. It was a horribly large field, Mattis thought, you couldn't even see the other end, it went over a ridge and disappeared.

Mattis turned to the farmer and said in a disgruntled tone : 'What's the use of having so many turnips?'

He stood there sullen and lost.

'What, already? Before we've even begun?' said the farmer. The words sounded meaningless, but to Mattis they were clear enough, and he hung his head.

41

'Shall I do these?' he said, hurriedly changing the subject. He pointed to the rows of turnips just in front of his feet.

The farmer nodded.

'I imagine you've done this sort of work before, Mattis, so I expect you know how much room you need between the plants you leave to grow?'

The farmer no doubt felt obliged to say this, for thinning out was an important job which could well determine the yield, and his reward for his labours.

'How could I ever have become nearly forty without knowing a thing like that?' said Mattis. 'I'm only three years off,' he added. In a situation like this you had to be tough. He was quite proud of his reply.

'True enough,' answered the farmer, 'but I asked how much room *you've* been told to leave between the plants. Perhaps you'd like to show me?'

Mattis pointed, quite haphazardly.

'No,' said the farmer, 'you must have learnt from someone who didn't know much about it. *This* is how it ought to be done.'

Once again Mattis hung his head.

The young man and the girl exchanged glances. They'd arranged it so they could work side by side. Mattis was given two rows between the girl and the farmer himself, much to his satisfaction.

'One two three, go!' shouted the young man. 'Who'll be the first to reach the other end?'

He looked at the girl and laughed. They liked to smile at one another, these two, and look into each other's eyes. Mattis had felt a little suspicious the moment he noticed.

But now it was simply a question of getting started. Mattis tried to copy the others, and be just as quick in his movements. There were weeds everywhere, on the sides of the furrow and in between the turnips on the top. Now

42

they were to be pulled up and left to the mercy of the scorching sun. The turnips, too, were standing much too close together, so that a lot of them had to be pulled up. Mattis had to manage all this quickly and accurately, both with the hoe, and, where they were difficult to get at, with his hands.

He was nervous. He simply couldn't.

Soon it would probably be the same old story, his thoughts would get out of control while he was working, confusing him and hampering his ability to work.

No sooner had he thought about it than it happened; his fingers got confused, did the opposite of what he wanted, and slowed him down.

To the left of him someone cleared his throat. It was the farmer himself, bending down over his turnip seedlings, thinning them out with loving care.

Mattis was on his guard at once. Of course it didn't necessarily mean anything. People sometimes clear their throats for no reason at all.

But Mattis grew more and more nervous, his fingers fumbled among the plants and pulled up the wrong ones. The hoe didn't work properly in his hands, it was too stiff.

'I'm not used to this hoe,' he told the farmer, 'the handle's too long.'

'Well I wouldn't bother with it then,' said the farmer, 'you might just as well use your fingers. You can do the work better, too, using your fingers.'

'I'm glad you said that,' said Mattis in a heartfelt tone. He sensed friendly support in the farmer's words, support he needed against the two young people.

He kept up with the young man and the girl, too, for the first few yards. After all, he had ten fingers to weed with. The two of them were marvellous at keeping the same speed. They were even enjoying themselves, despite the hard work. Mattis had realized some time ago that

43

they were sweethearts. It was a pity, but fun to watch as well, and exciting. Mattis didn't ever remember having been so near a pair of sweethearts before.

The girl looked across at Mattis with eyes full of happiness. He had nothing to fear from *her*, her gaze was overflowing with the love she felt for the young man by her side. She laughed at everything he said. At last she turned to Mattis who was waiting anxiously. He was filled with a delight no words could express. The round, laughing face of a girl was beaming happily at him.

'It's a good thing you came along,' she said, 'all the more of us to cope with this awful field.' She seemed to mean it, too. And Mattis was ready to believe every word she said. To gain confidence. He grew bolder, and in an effort to thank her and please her he produced his trump card : 'Have you ever heard about the flight of a woodcock?' he asked her. The rows they were standing in were so close to each other that he was able to say it quietly, confidentially.

She replied quickly without giving it a thought : ''Course I have. What of it?'

'Oh, nothing.'

The thought that occupied Mattis more than anything else was : Now I'm talking to a girl. And maybe this is just the beginning.

'But I don't suppose you've ever had a woodcock flying right over your house?' he went on and for once felt on safe ground.

The girl shook her head. At the same time she was busy weeding, tearing up handfuls of thick, healthy goose-foot and flinging them away to wither in the scorching sun. Mattis was working as best he could in the row next to her. And meanwhile they talked.

'I don't suppose the woodcock flies right over *your* house either,' she said innocently.

'Who knows,' said Mattis.

Inwardly he was bubbling with excitement.

'Oh well then,' said the girl absentmindedly, her attention on the weeding and the young man on the other side of her.

After that nothing more was said about it. Mattis felt he'd succeeded in mentioning it very cunningly. He liked this girl—but she had her boy-friend alongside her, so he mustn't talk to her too much. He knew there were very strict rules about such things. Just one or two more words, then he'd stop.

'I—' he began, but lost contact with her. The young man was there now, pinching her bare leg. She was lost to Mattis at once. It was as if there were no one at all on this side of her.

Well, it turned out a bit differently from the dream, he said to himself. But it's probably just as well nothing more came of this, things being what they are.

The worst of it was that all this thinking cost him a lot of time. The young couple were pushing ahead of him now. Before long they were quite a way ahead of him, so all he could see was their backs. Mattis gave a start and turned towards the farmer himself. Then he gave another start : the farmer was doing *three* rows. To begin with he'd had two, like the young couple.

'How come you're doing three rows?' Mattis blurted out.

'Well,' said the farmer hesitatingly, 'it's easier for us to keep together like that—at least that's *one* way of doing it,' he said, tearing up goose-foot and hemp nettles galore.

Mattis didn't give the matter any more thought, but moved closer to the farmer and said almost in a whisper : 'I think those two are sweethearts. At least it looks like it.'

The farmer nodded.

45

'Perhaps you knew already?'

'Yes,' said the farmer. 'That's why I got hold of them,' he explained, winking at Mattis. He too lowered his voice: 'They're the best ones for thinning out turnips, you know. They don't notice how dull and heavy the work is. Of course it's different with people like you and me.'

What a wise man he was. Mattis almost felt frightened of being near him—although he realized the farmer had been kind to him today, was really being friendly towards him the whole time. No, he wasn't afraid, he could talk to this man, and understood perfectly that the work could seem heavy and dull.

'Yes,' he said, '*we* know what it's really like thinning out turnips.'

'Not yet we don't,' the farmer replied firmly. 'Surely we're not tired already are we? When we've only just started?'

Once again Mattis had to hang his head.

'No, of course not,' he said.

Although the farmer was doing three rows he was now moving quickly ahead. Then he changed back to two again which was the normal thing. After that it didn't take him long to pull right away from Mattis.

Mattis shouted helplessly: 'Are you leaving me behind?'

'Got to, I'm afraid,' said the farmer. 'You'll just have to follow on as quickly as you can.'

'But you can see how hard I'm working.'

'Hm,' said the farmer stooping down over the goose-foot.

And Mattis was alone. Hm, was the last thing the farmer had said. How was he to take it? Mattis grew nervous again, the usual confusion between thoughts and work increased. His rows trailed behind like a tail growing longer and longer. Lazy-tail, that's what he seemed to

46

have heard people call it. This isn't a lazy-tail, he said to himself, I just can't work any faster.

But there hung the tail, and to somebody as touchy about such things as Mattis the disgrace was painfully obvious. His rows were covered with shiny green weeds, but on either side lay clean, brown rows, with an even line of turnips along the top.

If only it had been possible to stop the others somehow so that he didn't get left behind. Things were going very wrong. The farmer was a man with drive, he'd overtaken the young couple, and soon all three of them would be going over the little ridge and disappearing down the slope on the other side.

There they went.

Mattis was left behind. It was as if he was standing all alone in the field. Lonely and sweating. The sun was scorching and his shirt stuck unpleasantly to his back.

All these turnips, he thought, full of disgust. What's the good of them all? As if turnips were the only thing in the world!

Mattis had long since stopped stooping down, he had begun crawling forwards on his knees. His fingers wouldn't do as they were told, they misunderstood his thoughts, and now and again they held up the work completely.

He recognized it all so well from past experience, he expected it. He carried on as best he could, but his thoughts went darting in all directions. After a while he noticed that he was pulling up turnips instead of goosefoot. He gave a start, got up on his feet and stood trembling.

Am I going—

No, no.

There were the farmer and the young couple coming back from the other side of the ridge, each busy with two new rows. As they appeared the girl lifted her head a little

47

and gave a quick wave to Mattis who stood there helpless and forlorn. Nothing but a brief wave in between pulling up weeds. But to him it made all the difference.

I'll reward her for that, he vowed, surely that isn't against the rules. They'd be passing one another in a little while and he'd have the chance of telling her, boy-friend or no boy-friend.

For a while, too, his hands did what was expected of them. He crawled forward on his knees. pulling up weeds this time, and not turnips. Now that they were moving towards one another, it looked as if Mattis was really getting some speed up; the distance between them was rapidly growing smaller. But Mattis had stopped altogether; he was lost in contemplation of the young couple.

They were real lovers, there was no doubt about it.

No wonder the farmer was pleased with them, and gave them a brief smile from time to time. It couldn't only be the work he was thinking of—they made it pleasant for everyone in the field. They were laughing and chatting, and working properly the whole time as well. Now and then they managed to get really close to one another, and Mattis noticed carefully many small things that they did then, things it might be useful to know.

This was what real sweethearts were like, then. The lucky farmer was keeping up with them, in the rows he was doing. Between the three of them and Mattis there was now a dark patch that had been weeded. His two rows lay in front of him, ugly and neglected.

But he couldn't help it : he had to watch this sparkling young couple and listen to their talk; their bubbling joy; their strange eyes. They were right opposite him now. Rippling laughter, forcing its way through all the grind and toil.

Mattis got to his feet.

'However much you're sweethearts, I want to—' he

began frantically, looking straight at the beautiful girl. But then he got stuck.

The others waited in surprise, both the girl and the young man. They weren't laughing, either. Though he didn't realize it, Mattis himself prevented this by the adoration on his face and in his voice.

The farmer, too, had quietly stopped where he was.

They waited in vain. At last the farmer said in a soft voice : 'Well, go on then, Mattis.'

The girl said nothing, nor did the young man, they were both waiting anxiously.

They waited in vain, all of them. Mattis never got any further with what he'd started saying—but all the same it was as though he'd managed to establish some kind of contact and was no longer left struggling all alone. There was so much more he'd wanted to say, and in a different way, but as usual it had gone from him, had got mixed up with all kinds of other things.

'Because you are, aren't you?' he said finally, continuing where he'd left off.

'Yes,' replied the girl, 'we are.'

'Yes, that's how it ought to be for all of us,' he blurted out before he realized what he was saying.

'That can be put right, surely,' said the girl, giving him a casual nod.

I could have told my dream to this girl from beginning to end, he thought.

'Well, there's nothing more,' he mumbled embarrassed. 'I mean, nothing more I wanted to say.'

'Pity,' said the girl.

'Let's get cracking,' said the young man, reminding the two of them that he was there as well, and that there was a weeding race on.

Behind them the lucky farmer who had these two splendid workers was chuckling. He obviously took no account of Simple Simon, nobody did.

'All right, all right,' said the girl in reply. 'I can hear you.'

Ping, said a quiet voice inside Mattis, directed at the young man who'd received this rap over the knuckles.

They all started working again.

The sun was getting hotter and hotter. In the furrows frail, uprooted plants lay withering and dejected. A warm smell rose from the soil.

Mattis looked behind him at the farmer. Was he feeling tired and fed up? he wondered. Pretty unlikely, a strong, clever man like him. Mattis was both tired and thirsty by now, had lost all control over his fingers. The girl had revived his flagging spirits, but they sank again under the pressure of a job he couldn't cope with. And now the three of them were moving away again, this time behind him, giving the whole place a sad and desolate air. Every now and again his thoughts got confused, and he found he was pulling up turnips instead of weeds, and had to stop.

When at long last he reached the ridge and had to work his way down the other side, he felt even lonelier. The others seemed to be gone for good.

His shiny green rows stretched out like a challenge. He dug about, thinking : I must at least earn my food. After that he sat down for a while. Nobody could see him, and the confusion he was in upset all the movements of his hands. Besides, it was so nice to sit down when you were tired.

When he saw the three of them appearing over the ridge again a little later, he gave a start. Already! He started fumbling about, destroying a lot of good turnips. But still, it was nice that someone was coming. It was so desolate on this side of the ridge. The young couple weren't chirping quite as much as before, but all the same. And the farmer didn't seem to be tired. When you've got a field as large as this you don't get tired, you just get on with the work. He didn't even look up.

A very odd sound made them start: it was Mattis.

'Please stop!' he cried. It was a shout forcing its way out.

The farmer straightened up quickly, dashing the sweat off his brow with a hand covered in earth. He was certainly sweating.

'What's the matter, Mattis?'

Mattis was in a bad way. Although he hadn't finished one trip across the field, he felt worn out. The dust had formed a faint moustache under his nose. The others might look the same, but it didn't seem to matter on them. Hesitantly Mattis walked over to the farmer.

'Can't you see I'm getting left behind?'

'Well, what of it?' the farmer replied reluctantly.

'Did you realize?'

'Yes, yes,' said the farmer, dismissing the topic.

'I'm afraid I don't like complicated work like this," said Mattis in a serious tone.

'No, I suppose not,' answered the farmer, bending right down over the turnips.

Mattis was tempted to ask: Do you want me to stop? But he didn't. The farmer mumbled something to himself. The young couple took advantage of the pause to give each other a pinch or two.

Suddenly the farmer asked straight out: 'Do you want us to do your rows?'

A grey cloud drifted in front of his eyes. Something familiar from his old life, just as it was before the woodcock arrived.

'Not yet,' he answered stiffly.

'All right then.'

The farmer stooped over his hoe.

Mattis started to walk back to the place where he'd been working, but on the way he gave the girl a glance, a glance imploring her to do something to help and comfort him—after all, she was so young and happy, and she had a boy-friend.

He cleared his throat, as a sign that he needed help quickly.

She seemed to understand. She smiled at him as if reminding him: Here we are, you and I, waving to each other in the field.

That was all he needed. What was more, he heard it so distinctly that he put it into words and repeated it.

'Yes, here we are, you and I, in the field,' he said, just as warmly and gently, but not as secretively as she had done.

'Yes, we are,' said the girl.

It was really true. She was standing looking at him, awkward and helpless though he was. She was quite spellbound.

'One two three, go!' said the young man, giving her leg a pinch—this seemed to be his favourite pastime—and at once the girl became completely absorbed by her boy-friend again.

'Yes,' said the farmer too.

The farmer with the big field. They glanced at him quickly and knew what he meant; off we go!

Once more the three of them moved quickly past Mattis. He looked across at them. They seemed to have all the things he longed for: the three things. These people were nothing *but* the three things. They were full of them and yet they didn't give them a thought, weren't even aware of them, as far as he could see. How could they go around, calmly thinning out a turnip field?

He lay flat on his stomach pulling things up, his thoughts roaming wildly. Help me, he thought.

But his thoughts flitted aimlessly as before. Although he meant to pull up weeds, he pulled up turnips.

Nobody *wants* to help me, that's the trouble, he thought, and colours began dancing in front of his eyes.

The precious turnips infuriated him. They lay there puny and threadlike when he'd pulled up the things they were resting against. Mattis wanted to shout abuse at them in his wretchedness, wanted to call them dreary little weaklings, not worth lying here for, feeling miserable. His thoughts wandered to and fro. This was what always happened when he tried to work—nothing had changed. And *that* was what was really bothering him today : no change, just the same old routine.

Thank goodness! There was a call from the others on the far side of the ridge. 'Mattis!'

It was the farmer himself, the wise one. The beautiful one and the strong one said nothing, but they were there all right. All the three things were there.

'Is it lunchtime?' Mattis shouted back, quick as lightning.

'Yes, come along!' cried the farmer, still out of sight. The pleasant calls rang back and forth across the ridge. Mattis was already on the move.

Mattis still had a bit of his first two rows left to do. But the end was at least in sight, so it might have been worse, he reflected, feeling a little better now he was on his way to a good meal.

The others didn't say a word about his poor work when he joined them to leave the field. Not a single word was said—but Mattis was sure they were thinking of nothing else. He bottled it up inside him for a while, but in the end he exploded: 'You can come out with whatever it is you're thinking!' he said to them as they washed their dirty hands in the stream.

'What is it we're thinking, then?' asked the young man. It was the first time he had spoken to Mattis.

'I know all right,' said Mattis who was in a state of great agitation and had to go on tormenting himself.

'Ah well,' said the farmer, 'let's go back to the house and get something to eat. Have a little rest and—'

They washed their hands in a clear little stream that flowed near the edge of the field. The girl washed her hands in the same pool as Mattis. Down in the water, made turbid by the mud, their hands touched for a brief moment as they plunged them in. A shock ran right through him. Gradually the running water swept the pool and the hands in it clean again. But now he dared not go anywhere near her.

The girl looked at him, and he had no time to think.

'It was almost like touching an electric fence,' he blurted out.

Afterwards he thought he had put it rather well, but all she did was to turn away. Surely she wasn't laughing? Her boy-friend was washing his hands near by, too, and when he'd finished he put his arm round her as if it were the most natural thing in the world—and in this way they walked across to the farm where the meal was waiting. Perhaps they weren't even tired. Mattis thought of the young man's arm bulging inside his shirt—to think he put the whole of it round her waist. That was how things ought to be.

'Hello, Mattis.'

It was the farmer's wife. She gave Mattis a friendly welcome. Her food was good and Mattis ate heartily. There's something to be said for this after all, he thought. The heavy meal made him tired and sleepy, so he lay

54

down on the grass outside. He didn't see what became of the young couple. He fell asleep.

11

When Mattis woke up after having lain asleep in the midday sun he was absolutely scorched. The first thing he noticed when his head cleared was the three turnip-thinners in that awful field. Far away in the distance they were stooping down over rows of turnips. And they had been there for a long time, that was obvious from the work that had been done.

They had left without waking him. The disgrace was probably no more than he deserved. As he stood there trying to face up to the situation, the farmer's wife came out of the house. She walked up to him and said without hesitation : 'It was me that told them not to wake you. He wanted to give you a shake, but you were so fast asleep I thought it'd be better to let you sleep on. It's a couple of hours since they went.'

Mattis blinked, not knowing what to say. The woman was friendly. And now he understood why he had left the road so suddenly and come up here this morning. The memory of this face was fixed in his mind, from a previous occasion. He had seen it once before.

'Perhaps you didn't get much sleep last night, either?' the woman asked, offering him a reasonable excuse.

'No, I didn't!' he said, 'I haven't slept for two nights. There's a woodcock begun a flight over our house.'

The way he said it made her start, but it was only for a brief moment, until she remembered who she was dealing with. He did not fail to notice it.

'Well I never,' she said quietly. 'In that case it's not surprising you need to catch up on some sleep. How did the flight start, then?' she asked patiently.

Mattis's face lit up.

'It just came. Late one evening. I've had such strange dreams since, too.'

'Have you now? Still, dreams are rather private things, don't you think, so we won't discuss them,' said the woman who had a lot to get on with.

She was a wise woman, he could see that. He looked uneasily in the direction of the turnip thinners sweating in the field. The woman understood what was bothering him.

'Now which would you rather,' she said, 'join the others in the field or come in with me and have a cup of coffee?'

'Oh, I'd rather have the coffee, I think,' he said, livening up.

'I think you made a wise choice,' said the woman.

'But it's fun watching the sweethearts, too,' said Mattis, trying to be honest.

'Yes, I'm sure, but we'll let the sweethearts get on with it, shall we, and drink our coffee.'

'Well, if that's all right.'

That's what women ought to be like, he thought, following her into the kitchen.

They had some good coffee. The woman asked what his sister was doing.

'Oh, working away at her sweaters as usual, you know.'

After this they sat in silence. Mattis felt awful thinking of Hege having to keep him.

'I'm a terrible eater, too,' he said. He mustn't lie to this woman. 'I eat up all she earns,' he said.

The woman didn't say anything. Just kept filling up his cup.

'Now she's turning grey, too,' he said.

The woman remained silent.

'It's not easy having me,' he said.

Then the woman got up, saying almost harshly: 'Do stop talking about this, Mattis.'

Stop talking about it? But he was longing to talk about himself and his problems. It wasn't often you had the chance of sitting and drinking good coffee and opening your heart to women.

'Well, if I can't I suppose I can't,' he said.

His voice was trembling.

The woman found an excuse for going into the next room, so that Mattis could be alone. When she came back he had hardly moved; he sat surrounded by baffling problems, waiting with an important question. He began: 'But I can *ask* you something, can't I?'

She nodded, but not very invitingly.

'Yes, you can ask. But we'll have to see whether I'll answer or not. If I can.'

Mattis asked: *'Why are things the way they are?'*

The woman shook her head. Nothing more. He didn't dare repeat the question. He waited patiently. Patient to all appearances, but inwardly he was frantic with impatience. He turned to her again. Once more she shook her head.

'More coffee?' she said.

He understood and yet he didn't. He shuddered. Stared down into an abyss of riddles.

'You bet,' he said, referring to the coffee.

'But now the woodcock's here?' he continued as though asking a question.

'Yes, that's a thing we've never had over our house,' said the woman quickly, happy at being able to talk about something like this. 'Now you stay there,' she said, and left him for a little while, giving his disturbing question time to sink back into the depths from which it came.

Time passed. Mattis sat where he was.

'I bet they're sweating now,' he said to the woman.

She was getting the next meal ready, it would soon be time for it.

'Do you think I ought to go and help?'

'Too late now. They'll be coming in very soon. You just stay put,' she said. She could see he didn't know what to do. 'They wouldn't even want you turning up now.'

There was an air of authority in her voice and in the expression on her face. The thought of meeting the others filled Mattis with dread and made him writhe in his chair. After a while the woman went out into the yard and called them home. How he wished he had been out there, washing his hands in the little pool.

There they were. The door was open. They hung around a bit outside. Mattis who had a keen sense of hearing was listening anxiously to see if anyone said Simple Simon. Yes, there it was. It was the young man who said it. Mattis didn't hear the rest. The three of them came in. Mattis sat full of anxiety. Shamefacedly he turned to the farmer : 'I meant to come and finish off what's left of my two rows, but I was asked in to coffee instead.'

The farmer nodded curtly. His back was tired, and he was no longer as friendly as he had been in the morning.

'We finished that bit of yours long ago,' he replied. 'We couldn't have that sort of thing left about.'

The sweethearts walked past Mattis as though he weren't there. They looked embarrassed.

'Come and have something to eat, Mattis,' said the farmer, dismissing the matter in spite of all that had happened.

'Yes, I'm jolly hungry,' Mattis replied. At the same time he groaned inwardly.

It was the two sweethearts that helped him at the table all the same. They were so young that he'd expected sidelong glances and sly grins, but they sat quietly, looking at him in a kindly way. No doubt the woman had told them how to behave before they came in. He'd known that kind of thing happen many times. Doesn't matter to me what the reason for it is, he said to himself, hastily turning his anxiety into a feeling of pleasure.

Pity, though, that the young couple were so tired now that they couldn't be sweethearts in the same way as they had been earlier in the day. It's a real shame! he thought. He felt a strong desire to talk to the girl about it, now while they sat opposite one another eating. He brought his gaze to rest upon her. Her freshly washed hands lay on the table. There was something friendly and likeable about her.

'Are you feeling tired?' he began. He decided to risk it. Without realizing it he had asked gently, like a mother, and everyone round the table looked at him in amazement. The girl turned red and could hardly answer.

'Yes,' she said in a quick, low murmur, drawn towards something she felt to be good and sympathetic, and which held her entranced.

They were all waiting for Mattis to continue, and he did : 'It's almost a pity to be sweethearts really, when you're tired!' he said. He sensed that things were going wrong and getting confused. But that was what he'd meant after all.

They were all able to laugh freely and continue eating again. Mattis had to laugh too. Had he been clever after all? His laughter was like the whinny of a horse, and that made the others laugh even more. Then it became very quiet, as after a sudden blow. What was it? No one knew.

They got up from the table. Work was over for the day,

and the farmer asked the sweethearts if they could come and help him again the next day.

'Suppose so,' they replied and left. Mattis sent a long glance after them. He wasn't likely to be coming back tomorrow, so he wouldn't be able to enjoy watching them.

'I don't suppose you want *me* tomorrow?' he forced himself to ask. The way things had gone that day it seemed almost brazen.

The farmer felt a bit uncomfortable as well.

'Not much point really, is there?' he said. It was difficult to avoid putting it like that. 'What do you feel about it yourself then? But let's settle up for today anyway.'

'No! I didn't do any work, you know I didn't.'

'Oh, but you must have your pay.'

'Well, for two rows, then,' said Mattis, almost frantically. 'But no more. See how much it is.'

It was a difficult moment for both of them. Mattis saw the woman glance quickly at her husband. The farmer said: 'All right, we'll leave it at that then. Two rows. Now we're all square.'

The farmer paid up and uttered a few customary words of thanks.

'Hm!' Mattis mumbled to himself.

'Anything the matter?'

'No. Just all square.'

All square, he mumbled to himself. These two impressive words sent a warm glow through him. That's how men speak to men.

He took his hat.

'Well, so much for that,' he said by the door. The farmer and his wife looked at him, a little hesitantly.

12

Back at home Hege was sitting outside with her work. She had chosen a place that gave her a view of the path down from the main road. Mattis caught sight of her the moment he came into the clearing. He thought she looked as insignificant as a little ball of wool.

From where he stood she seemed such a little thing. All huddled up. Nothing at all.

Wonder what it's like *inside* her, he thought. Clever thing she was. It filled him with respect. Might be like a volcano there, for all he knew.

She ought to have been the younger of them—he would have seen her while she was a tiny little mite then, and been able to spoon-feed her and watch food dribbling from the corners of her mouth. Yes, that ought to have been quite the other way round as well.

The shadows thrown by the trees began to grow longer. Evening was coming, and it was getting cool. Pleasant and refreshing when you'd been out in the heat and turmoil of the day.

Hege got up when he arrived.

'I suppose you've eaten?' she greeted him.

'You bet I have,' Mattis replied emphatically, pleased to be able to tell her about something he'd done well to-day. 'No shortage of food where I was,' he added.

Hege started asking where he'd been and what he'd been doing, she wanted to know all about how he'd spent the day. And there was nothing for it but to tell her.

'And I stayed there at the farm until now.'

'I see.'

If only he'd been able to put a whole day's pay down on the half-finished sweater.

'But things were all square,' he said quickly, 'I was paid on the dot.'

'What did you get then?'

She was impossible on things like this.

'The money for the two rows, of course! If things were all square. Otherwise it would have been all wrong.'

'I see,' said Hege.

'Well, you know what things being all square means, don't you? With all those sweaters you make.'

He became excited and his voice began to tremble. He went on hurriedly to tell Hege about the sweethearts.

'And then I asked the farmer's wife questions she just couldn't answer,' he said finally.

Hege said, irritated : 'Again? More questions?'

'Yes, that's the way she was,' said Mattis.

'Makes no difference, one day you'll have to stop it,' said his sister sternly.

'Why?'

'Because it's just silly,' said Hege bitterly.

He flinched and said no more. No mention was made of what he had asked the farmer's wife. Hege knew already.

But later that evening Hege said she would come and see his woodcock. He took this as her way of rewarding him for the unpleasant and difficult day he had spent working. He had come to regard the woodcock almost as his own creation. Hege followed him outside.

'It's a good thing you came to your senses,' he said.

Outside it was quiet, just the right weather. Mattis looked eagerly in every direction and listened, full of expectation.

The bird came, bringing with it all those things for

which there were no words. Hege felt it, too. A flash, a touch of the wing inside you, and it was gone again.

Hege didn't say anything, but her attitude seemed at least friendly. Mattis said, deeply moved : 'And it comes again and again.'

Now they could go to bed, Hege said, but he felt sure she was moved.

He laid his hand on her arm. Wanted to tell her that the house was different now, was somehow better than other houses, had been transformed. It was impossible to explain what he meant, but at least he could lay his hand on her arm.

'Now you've seen it,' was all he said. Without wanting to he made it sound as though he owned the bird. Hege, forgetting herself, said : 'Well, it isn't you who have brought it here, is it? Anyone'd think so, the way you're talking.'

A slap in the face. He stared at her, frightened. Saying that sort of thing at a moment like this. Then anger welled up inside him.

'What kind of a person are you! Always spoiling things!'

'Hush now.'

He was not going to be hushed, looked around for something he could somehow use against her. The first thing his eyes fell upon were the two withered aspen trees. He forgot all the promises of good behaviour he had made earlier, pointed to the trees : 'Do you see those? I'll tell you something : they've been named after the two of us. People never call them anything else! Now you know. It's not just my name that's been used, it's yours as well.'

He expected to see Hege wither away. But nothing happened. She simply said, quite unperturbed : 'Oh, so you know about that?'

He stared.

'I thought I was the only one of us who knew about it,' she said, patting him on the arm.

She stood there, the proudest person he'd ever known. A sudden change had come over her. She talked about the withered trees : 'What harm do they do us? None at all. A stupid boyish game like that. It's just childish.'

She grew in stature. And Mattis grew because he was standing next to her and was her brother, and because one of the withered tree-tops was his and could do him no harm.

All the same he couldn't entirely agree with her. It was much easier for her to say things like that. But it was comforting to listen to her, and the sight of her gave him strength. She looked straight into his eyes and said in a firm voice : 'And now we won't mention this again. Let the trees stay there as long as they like. It's no concern of ours.'

'Well, if that's how you feel about it,' said Mattis. There was no more for him to say.

13

Two days later Hege said :

'Mattis, I think you ought to try again now.'

It sounded almost like an order.

'Go out and work?'

'Ask for work at least. Seeing you managed so well last time.'

'Things are going to be different now,' he replied, and showed no sign of obeying her.

Hege said sharply : 'Well, can't you go somewhere or other while you're waiting for *that* to happen.'

It was early and it looked as though it was going to be a fine day. For two days Mattis had been sitting down on the shore, throwing stones and thinking. He had rowed about a bit and done some fishing, without catching anything, as usual. All Hege really wanted was to avoid seeing him sitting down there throwing those silly stones again and again. It wasn't because of the work—*that* wouldn't come to anything.

The sharp tone of her voice decided the issue.

'But not thinning out turnips!' he implored her.

'It doesn't matter to me, you know, as long as you come back with some money,' said Hege showing no mercy.

'It depends on my thoughts,' said Mattis, 'they decide in the end. Gosh, you're really a hard one,' he allowed himself to add.

'Oh, I'm sure it'll turn out all right,' said Hege. 'There are plenty of small jobs hereabouts for anyone who's prepared to do them.'

How keen she was to get rid of him. She was more stubborn than before, more impatient, he told himself, heaping silent accusations upon her.

Where was he to go? He had set off as Hege had told him. The farm he had been at last time was out of the question, he was finished there for good. No doubt they were still at the same kind of work, too. He drifted over towards them. Yes, there they were, the three of them. Just come out into the huge field. There was still a bit of it left to do. It felt almost odd to be walking down the road past them, he knew them so well since that day, had shared so many experiences with them. The sweethearts seemed to be full of the joy of morning.

Were they glancing down at him on the road?

No.

Give a little wave, he pleaded. It would be something

65

he could treasure for years to come. The girl, of course. He didn't want the men to wave, that would have embarrassed him. But the girl. No, she didn't seem to notice anything but the pinching.

A little farther on two small girls were sitting on the grass just above the road. Sitting safely on the other side of the fence with their toys, chattering and playing with dolls, so young that they were free from sin. They were prattling busily to each other, but even so one of them found time to ask, her round blue eyes resting on him, and with a voice full of song: 'Where are you off to, Simple Simon?'

Full of song and not at all curious, a question asked for the sake of asking. Of course the children knew their nearest neighbours, living as close to the road as they did. So Mattis, too, was a familiar sight.

Take it easy now, he said to himself, they're too young to know what they're saying.

'Nowhere special,' he replied.

They asked no further questions, it didn't make the slightest difference to them where he was going.

All the same he hurried away from them. And some shining cars rushing past restored his courage. It was so easy meeting cars you didn't know. No one sitting inside them knew he was Simple Simon. He looked straight at the people sitting inside—they'd probably think he was as clever as they were.

He trudged past one farm after another. He ought to have started work by now. But when he came to a gate he stopped to see how his legs felt: he had a test he had invented on a previous occasion when he had been in the same helpless predicament.

'If you want to go up there, then I'm sure I'll feel a jerk,' he said to his legs, and waited.

No, there was no jerk in the direction of this farm, his

legs had more sense. He tried time and time again this morning, with the same negative result at each new gate.

But what'll Hege say about my going on like this, I wonder?

The fact was that Hege knew nothing about the leg-test, it was a secret. She was slow in accepting things like that.

Finally he came to the store—and this was really what had been in his mind the whole time. There was no need to use the test there either, for the store stood right by the road, like a trap for everyone to fall into. It was close to the lake, too, by a kind of pier.

Inside you could get boiled sweets. Mattis was fond of boiled sweets. The storekeeper had never laughed at him either, when he behaved helplessly.

There was nobody that Mattis knew in the store at this time of day, just a few cyclists, young holidaymakers in shorts, drinking lemonade. Mattis knew he mustn't stare at them too long. He forced himself to stop. He dug into his pocket for money and found the fifty øre he knew was there.

'A bag of boiled sweets,' he said casually, as if it were something he did several times a week.

The storekeeper asked as a matter of routine : 'Camphor drops?'

The storekeeper knew his habits. It was nice to have the strangers in the shop listening. Mattis was grateful for this short, safe conversation.

'Yes, the usual,' he said. Anyway he had a more important kind of question today.

'Do you know how a woodcock can change its path and go straight across a house where it hasn't been before?' he asked. It was a complicated question he'd learnt by heart on the way.

'Woodcocks don't change their path, do they?' said the

storekeeper. 'If you get a flight in a new place, then it's most likely one of last year's young cocks starting up on his own, I should think.'

While the storekeeper was talking he was digging down into the tin of camphor drops with a little shovel. A delightful yellow glow filled the shiny sides of the tin.

'Do you think so?' said Mattis, downcast.

'Nothing wrong with that is there? Is it something you've seen quite recently, then?'

'Oh no—not the way you mean, I don't think. There's nothing special about what you're saying. You mustn't make things out to be less important than they are when they really are important!'

He took the first boiled sweet.

Just then one of the cyclists said :

'Hell, look at those clouds! We'll be having a storm before long, that's for sure.'

Mattis gave a start and almost swallowed his sweet. Looking out of the window he, too, could see the dark bank of clouds climbing up over the ridge. The sun was still shining.

'Is there going to be a thunderstorm?' he asked frightened. His words were directed straight at the cyclist who stood there tanned and hairy.

The stranger looked at him a little surprised, but answered bitterly, talking to his pretty companion rather than to Mattis : 'Yes, there's going to be a terrific thunderstorm. And us looking forward to a nice trip.'

Nothing in the store interested Mattis any longer. There's going to be a thunderstorm, home, home, was the one thought in his mind. His hiding place was far away, and that was where he had to go.

He rushed out of the store. Through the half open door he heard the storekeeper saying something about him in reply to a question from the cyclist. Once more someone had misjudged his keen ears. He who could hear through walls and at a greater distance than anyone else—with all the practice he had listening for things that he wasn't supposed to hear.

'He is a bit simple,' the storekeeper was saying inside.

The storekeeper, too. Mattis would never have believed it. But why not? he had to ask himself at once. He's only telling the truth. He's a bit simple. All right. And a moment later he heard : 'But he's got a plucky sister, she's the one who keeps things going.'

Fortunately the door banged to, so he was spared the rest of the conversation. Perhaps that was all they said. He doesn't do a stroke of work, that fellow. Perhaps they said that too.

Well, for the time being this was overshadowed by the dark cloud and his fear of the thunderstorm. The important thing now was to get home and under cover in a safe place. He hurried along as quickly as he could, the bag of sweets clutched in his hand. The sun was still shining, intensely, as it always did before a storm.

Just behind him a car hooted angrily and he flung himself into the side of the road like a bundle of rags. The car must have braked hard and as it went gliding past, someone said through the open window : 'Don't walk in the middle of the road, you damned fool!'

It was an angry and a frightened voice. Mattis saw a pair of angry eyes looking at him out of the window. A complete stranger.

'It was touch and go,' said the shaken voice in the window. 'You could easily have been knocked flat, the way you're dithering about.' Then the window was wound up, and aiming a blast of poisonous exhaust at Mattis, the car sped away.

Swallowing great gulps of the exhaust Mattis staggered on, keeping close to the side of the road. He realized the man would have said exactly the same to anybody. He had shouted in fear. He was a stranger, and had no idea who he was talking to. Mattis told himself this over and over again, and as he did so, he suddenly realized that he was protected from hundreds of millions of people who knew absolutely nothing about him. It was as though a friendly haze lay between them and him. It was a comforting thought: countless numbers of people had no idea he was a simpleton.

But now he was running to beat the thunderstorm. He had seen many different kinds of thunderstorms. Some came on all of a sudden, others took their time and rumbled a good while before getting dangerous. Others stayed in the distance the whole time, they were heading somewhere else. There were no fixed rules. The clouds today were only coming over slowly. Mattis felt almost sure he'd get home in time.

The child who had called to him earlier was nowhere to be seen. But the three of them in the field were still digging away.

Will she wave?

No.

She must be tired.

But I won't think about it. There's going to be a thunderstorm soon, and you mustn't think about that sort of thing then. Don't even feel like thinking about it. That's the way it is with thunder.

All of a sudden he bumped into a man he vaguely knew. At least, he used to talk to him when they met, and he felt quite at ease with him. The man raised his hand, as if Mattis were a bus he wanted to stop.

'Wait a moment! You're in a bit of a hurry, aren't you, Mattis?'

'Well, you can see the storm, can't you?' said Mattis gravely.

'What storm?'

'There's going to be a thunderstorm very soon, can't you see? And home's the best place then.'

The man seemed to know how Mattis felt about thunder. He looked up at the clouds: 'I don't think you need worry. Those aren't thunder clouds, they're already thinning out, look!'

Mattis shook his head and refused to believe it. It had probably only been said to comfort him. A terrific thunderstorm, that's what the cyclist in the shop had said, and that was no doubt nearer the truth.

'What did I say? Look there, Mattis!'

Just as they stood there the clouds lifted and a patch of blue sky appeared over the edge of the mountains. The whole threat of thunder was gone, they were no longer storm-clouds. There was glorious blue sky just underneath.

'There you are,' said the man, 'it's only light cloud, and that means fine weather; it's melting away altogether now.'

Mattis drew a long sigh of relief.

'Like a sweet?' he said, full of gratitude.

And the man went on his way, sucking the yellow sweet.

Mattis returned to his usual walking pace. But it was so late in the day that it was no good looking for work now, he decided. He was not entirely happy at the prospect of having to return home to Hege and give an account of his attempts to get work. No sooner was the threat of thunder gone than he was faced with his old, familiar, nagging conscience.

He was by the path leading down to their little house. The withered tree-tops rose into the air. He never even looked at them.

No, he never even looked at them. Something unusual

happened that made him forget everything. As he came down the path—what was it he saw :

A bird.

There was a big, shining bird standing right in the middle of the path.

An unfamiliar bird. Its head raised high and turned towards Mattis who was coming down the path.

Who's this? he thought, spellbound.

He felt strange and empty inside. He stood quite still—and the bird stood quite still. *What is it I'm seeing?*

The bird stood there, but it couldn't stay any longer now it had been seen—it rose. On silent wings it disappeared among the trees. It wasn't the woodcock, it was a much larger bird, and very different, too, from the woodcock. And what was it doing here?

What's going on? he thought. Anything the matter with Hege! It was the only thing he could think of. He ran down the path to find out.

No. He soon caught sight of Hege, in the place where she usually sat on the look-out for him whenever he'd gone off somewhere. She was like a little bundle on the steps. Her fingers were moving busily. He sensed rather than actually saw this from where he was.

Mattis went down to her and said, wide-eyed : 'Who is it up there?'

She gave him a quick glance, didn't understand.

'What's the matter with you?'

'There's a strange bird up there,' he stuttered.

She went on working again. It was as if he wanted to stop these knitting needles, just for a little while; deeply moved he said : 'I've seen a wonderful big bird! It was walking around just up the path here.'

'Really,' she replied, rather curtly. All the same her tone wasn't as blunt as usual. There must have been something in his voice that told her how beautiful the bird had been. And that is was for somebody in their house it was beautiful. A silence followed. An unexpected pause. Something that had no name.

Mattis explained :

'It flew off almost before I had a chance to see it.'

There wouldn't be long to wait for it now, he thought, the impatient question as to why he was back as early as this when he was supposed to be at work. Best to take the bull by the horns.

'I just came back home, there didn't seem to be any work. I knew it would be like that anyway. And somebody said there was going to be a thunderstorm as well. But that didn't come to anything either.'

'No,' said Hege.

'But a girl I know waved to me,' he said. He translated his wish into reality then and there. It *was* real, he felt.

'Really,' said Hege.

She wasn't angry, she was moved. The shining bird had been reflected so beautifully in his face.

14

In the morning he thought, full of emotion.

Today it's me and the woodcock.

He couldn't explain how. Nor did he need any explanation. After all, there were streaks in the air above the house—left by the woodcock flying across while he was asleep, last night and every night now. It seemed almost wicked to sleep.

The more Mattis thought about the woodcock, the more he felt sure something good was going to happen. Something different. That was why the woodcock was flying across here morning and night, but always while people were hidden away inside their houses.

This made good sense, he felt. He himself could go outside and sit there watching, following the flight through the air as often as he liked. It was the woodcock and him.

Today was a new day with the bird.

Mattis was full of the woodcock. He couldn't resist telling Hege about it again and again. Hege was tired of it, but he felt he could twist his words so that she didn't realize what he was talking about, and yet find an outlet for his emotions.

Early in the morning, while Hege was getting him his breakfast, he said to her: 'It's away and back with me now.'

'What do you mean?' she asked patiently.

'Like this.'

With his finger he drew lines in the air above his head, in the same direction as the woodcock had been flying.

Hege was already busy with her next task. Always on the go. Mattis would very much have liked to share with her the things he was thinking and feeling at the moment, but Hege was blind, unable to see them.

'Wait, Hege, there's such *a lot* just now."

'Well, be quick then,' she said.

'How little you know about things.'

He said it in a friendly way and half afraid; after all he was talking to one of the clever ones.

'Yes, so you say,' Hege replied.

'Streaks hither and thither,' he said.

'And while you're asleep,' he said.

'Every single night,' he said, rounding the whole thing off.

She looked at him as at a grown-up now, and then she

said something: 'You're lucky, seeing things the way you do. I don't, I can tell you.'

She had stopped now, wasn't simply rushing off to her eight-petalled roses. Today once again she had heard a tone in his voice that made her pause.

'How do you see things, then?' he asked, forgetting himself. Spoilt the moment completely. She gave a start, even though she was really to blame.

But inwardly Mattis was bursting with song: him and the woodcock. He felt an urge to walk through the little wood, right underneath the invisible streaks in the sky. That was his path, a path full of joy. He wasn't disappointed this time, either. After a little while he had to stop.

You are you, a voice inside him seemed to be saying, at least that was what it sounded like to him.

It was spoken in the language of birds. Written in their writing.

He was standing by a dried-up patch of bog right underneath the woodcock's path, standing looking spellbound, reading a message or whatever it was that had been left there for him.

In the smooth brown surface of the marshy soil were the paint imprints of a bird's feet. A number of tiny, deep round holes had been dug as well. The woodcock had been there. The deep holes had been made by the woodcock's beak which it thrust down into the ground to dig up morsels of food, or sometimes just to prick out messages.

Mattis bent down and read what was written. Looked at the graceful dancing footprints. That's how fine and graceful the bird is, he thought. That's how gracefully my bird walks over the marshy ground when he's tired of the air.

You are you, that was what was written.

What a greeting to receive!

He found a twig and pricked an answer in an empty space on the brown surface. He didn't use ordinary letters; it was meant for the woodcock, so he wrote in the same way as the birds.

The woodcock's bound to notice it next time he's here. I'm the only one who comes here and the only one who writes.

It was a quiet, well-hidden spot. Impossible to imagine a better meeting-place. Tall trees stood round the little patch of bog, and the sunshine found its way into a small clearing, falling thickly and warmly on to the marshy ground and drying it up so that graceful, shy creatures could dance upon it.

Ought he to settle down here for the rest of the day and the evening, and wait for the bird to come and perhaps land right beside him?

It was tempting, but he pushed the idea firmly aside. He didn't dare. After all, the bird might get frightened— and something might be spoilt that mustn't be spoilt for anything in the world.

There was a greeting here now. That would have to do.

Tomorrow he would come back and see how the woodcock had got on with reading it. He went home whistling to himself, but said nothing—Hege couldn't understand things like this.

15

Off he went the next day full of excitement, and he wasn't disappointed. Not far away from his own writing the beak had pricked out a new message.

Mattis had expected this, but it had such an effect on him that he had to sit down on a stone.

Something really had been started between them.

And what did the bird say, in its wonderful language?

Mattis was in no doubt. It was about great friendship. Prick, prick, prick. Eternal friendship, that was what it meant.

He brought out the twig and solemnly pricked that he felt the same.

It was easy to express oneself in bird language. There was so much they were going to tell each other. There were more footprints here now. To Mattis it looked like dancing. Something had made the solitary bird dance.

But I mustn't stay here spying.

Mattis looked around him and said aloud: 'Great things.'

He used ordinary human speech. It felt coarse and commonplace. He would have liked to have started using bird language for good—to have gone back home to Hege and never spoken in any other way. Then she might have begun to understand some of the things that were at present hidden from her.

But he didn't dare, he had a fair idea of what would happen. Most likely they'd lock me up. They'd refuse to have anything to do with the finest of all languages, they'd laugh at it.

But with joy still bubbling through him he bent down and made a few more pricks. He could have filled the whole patch at this moment. But he mustn't do that— there had to be room left for the woodcock as well. Each day they were going to come flitting in here with light, dancing steps, to prick down all that was in their hearts.

The third day after the discovery it was the same, and the fourth day, too. Hege asked what he was doing over in the woods so often?

'Hm!' he said.

She didn't pursue the subject.

He felt an ever-growing temptation to lie in wait for the bird, but managed to resist it. He waited impatiently for each new day to begin.

On the fifth day there was no fresh greeting for him. What had happened? And weren't the woods quieter than usual too?

Inside him the words were painfully taking shape : the woodcock is dead.

No! No!

After four days of exchanging written messages he had become so engrossed in it all that he pictured terrible disasters as soon as there was no new message in the bog. All the same he pricked down something of his own before he went home. In the evening he sat outside the house waiting for the woodcock to arrive. Hege was asleep.

Soft, rainy air, just right. A sudden realization shot through him : One day the woodcock won't be flying across here any more. And one day there won't be a woodcock any more.

'Who's moaning about disaster?' he said with sudden confidence into the rainy air, for there came his missing bird, familiar and wonderful, following the same path, uttering the same cries. Mattis only just managed to stop himself rousing Hege from her sleep.

When he got to the meeting place the following day there was a new message for him, too.

That's the way it is with us, he thought.

And there was still an empty patch waiting to be covered with pricks and dancing toes.

16

But only a couple of days later Mattis began to feel ill. All of a sudden. He kept on wandering in and out of the house. When Hege started asking questions he replied: 'It's my stomach, sort of. But only sort of.'

'Is it something you've eaten, or is it the weather?'

'Neither the one nor the other,' he replied, wandering outside again.

The woodcock was in grave danger, that was what it was.

That morning he'd met a youngster up on the road who had asked if it was true that there was a woodcock flying right across his house? Yes, yes there was, Mattis had replied, happy that someone should ask. Up till now he had had to force his news on people.

Then suddenly he felt a cold shudder go right through him, and regretted bitterly every word he'd said. From a sudden gleam in the youngster's eyes he realized that he'd been talking to a fowler.

'But it's stopped now! It's too late in the summer. I haven't seen it for a long time.'

The youngster had just laughed—he knew better:

'D'you think I don't know when that sort of flight stops?'

Mattis's little lie fell flat to the ground. Mattis wanted to ask him not to do the bird any harm, but he was too slow, as he so often was when important things were at stake.

'Good-bye,' said the youngster quickly and set off with long, springy steps. He was tanned and strongly built, too, obviously one of those terrific workers everybody wanted to get hold of, and was willing to hire for the highest wage —and one of those the girls liked to have around.

But Mattis couldn't forget that gleam in the youngster's eyes. He was a fowler, and he might come back with a gun, and lie in wait for the woodcock at the edge of the forest, and simply shoot it down.

Perhaps that very evening. Was it any wonder his stomach felt peculiar?

He didn't want to discuss it with Hege, because she'd realize then that it was he himself who'd told the news to the fowler. He'd tried to comfort himself by saying that everyone knew about it by now, but it was no use. Today he'd told the news to a fowler who'd come for the sole purpose of questioning him. Mattis had realized too late.

His stomach felt worse as time went on. Outside it was turning into a nice warm evening. Overcast and the right smell of rain in the air, too. Mattis walked round the house, his face turned towards the bushes the whole time, as if to prevent someone from lying in wait there with a gun.

The whole thing seemed so hopeless. The woods round about might be hiding a hundred youngsters with guns, even though he couldn't see a single one. Yet he felt he had to go on trotting round the house, staring into the bushes, into the patches of darkness that began to gather there. More and more frightened of the invisible guns. There might well be lots of them.

No, no, no.

He circled round the house. What good did it do really? The birds flew high in the air, and he couldn't warn them until they were right over the roof—and not even then.

He gave a sudden start : the flight was beginning. His heart stopped beating.

The bird came.

One, two, three and away! Like a streak through Mattis. And the bird was allowed to continue its flight, no gun went off.

Perhaps it was just imagination after all? No, his fears were not dispelled. The gun was bound to be here somewhere, it just didn't go into action the first time.

Mattis continued his pointless journey, round and round. Then he shouted a warning 'Hey!' into the bushes. There was no reply.

'Hey!' he said in a louder voice.

No reply. But a moment later there came a sound of something snapping. A soft, dangerous sound.

Where was it? He hadn't heard where it came from. He shouted louder. He was certain there was someone there.

'Don't!' came his next shout, straight out.

'No one must do harm here!' he shouted.

A deathly silence hung over the forest.

There wasn't much time left now, either, before the woodcock was due back a second time.

'No!' he shouted. It sounded weak and breathless. He wasn't sure whether it was a warning to the hidden marksman not to commit a crime—or a warning to the flying bird not to come back this way. It was probably a bit of both.

Tonight the forest was changed beyond recognition. The forest where Mattis normally felt safe—tonight everything seemed sinister and uncanny. The evening sky was flooding the clearing with light, yet from somewhere in among the bushes the barrel of a gun was probably poking out. This had a paralysing and shattering effect on everything.

Mattis was just about to shout for the third time when he heard the swishing of a bird's wings. His mouth remained open without uttering a sound.

No—said a voice inside him, silent, like a kind of lament. Powerless.

Bang! came a thunderous report from the depths of the wood. So far away that Mattis hadn't spotted the place. And up in the air a bird gave a little cry.

Bang! came the muted echo from the hillside.

Mattis stood rooted to the spot. First the thunderous noise went rolling past him like a dark cloud, then the dead woodcock came toppling down from the evening sky and thudded to the ground a few steps from where he stood.

Still Mattis could not move. He tried to bring some order into his thoughts—they were in complete confusion. But there came a young lad rushing out from the bushes —and at the very same moment Mattis had his body under control, he jumped forward and picked up the warm bird that was filled with lead, smoothed its ruffled feathers and saw its dark eye.

The bird was looking at him.

No, no, don't think like that. Mustn't. This bird's dead.

Dead, why dead?

It looked at me first.

In the meantime the marksman had reached the clearing, he was half running, flushed with joy at his kill. It was the youngster he'd talked to earlier in the day all right, strong and happy.

Mattis was still standing with the bird in his hand.

'What a hit!' said the youngster, balancing the gleaming gun in his hand. 'I could only just see the bird, it was flying as swift as an arrow, so I just took a pot shot.'

Mattis made no reply.

'I don't suppose you understand this kind of thing,' said the youngster, 'but it was a damn good shot. And dead before it hit the ground, I see.'

Mattis stood there with the bird, looking lost. Silent. The hand with the bird dangled loosely at his side—it looked as if he'd forgotten what he was holding.

The youngster asked surprised : ' D'you think it's yours?'

Mattis said nothing.

'Give it here. I want to go home and show them what a good shot I am,' he said, winking and nodding at Mattis in a friendly way while he threw the gun over his shoulder and got ready to leave.

Mattis did not hand over the bird, made no move to obey, looked helplessly at the youngster. The youngster took a sudden step backwards.

'Why don't you say something?' he began again, no longer as happy as he had been when he came rushing up.

Mattis pulled himself together, he wanted to say something about the dark eyes that had looked at him—but then he noticed they were gone. They were shut. Nothing more to be said about them. He did not let go of the bird.

The youngster stood there, feeling cheated after his masterly shot. Mattis had taken the edge off his joy. He was not completely blind after all. He stood there full of youth and strength and vitality, but this silent simpleton frightened him.

He asked in a different tone : 'What's the matter, Mattis?'

No reply.

The youngster asked almost helplessly :

'Are you angry with me for this?'

Again no reply.

Mattis shook his head in despair. Should have said something. No or something. He looked down at the

83

ground, there was a spot of blood on the grass where the bird had come tumbling down. A little blood was still trickling from its beak. Mattis raised his head again and looked at the youngster without a word.

The youngster made no further attempt at conversation either. And he didn't take the bird from Mattis by force, despite his strength. He straightened up his gun and walked slowly out of sight, seemed to have come across something he didn't understand, and wouldn't easily be able to forget.

Mattis was left standing with the woodcock. Drops of blood trickled down into the grass from its long beak.

Alone again Mattis got back his power of speech; he mumbled in a low voice : 'Eyes shut.'

'No more.'

'Lead in its wing.'

He hadn't really noticed the youngster or what he'd been doing. Had no feeling of having done anything wrong in not handing over the bird. He walked towards the steps, dragged himself slowly through the entrance and into the living-room. There he placed the woodcock on the table.

This was no nightmare he was caught up in, then. It was real.

The woodcock lay with its eyes shut, full of heavy, hidden lead.

It had looked at him as he picked it up, there was no doubt.

He thundered on the door of the small room, forgetting how often he got a snappy answer when he arrived at the wrong moment. Hege must have fallen asleep long ago.

'You must get up, Hege. You must!' he said in a voice that was unrecognizable.

Hege was awake, she replied at once, reluctant and angry, no.

'But you must come, Hege. Something dreadful's happened.'

'Who to?'

He couldn't bear to say it : 'You'll see.'

The tone of his voice made her say at once : 'I'm coming, what is it then?'

She came straight out of bed, dishevelled and deep in her own thoughts, and frightened of whatever Mattis was so upset about. She didn't notice anything, but then Mattis pointed to the table where the bird was lying.

'You see that?'

'Ugh ! What's it doing on the table making such a mess,' she said in her familiar nagging tone when she saw the drops of blood on the table top. But she quickly checked herself when she noticed the expression on Mattis's face. She came closer. She was not so ignorant about the wild life of the forest as not to know what kind of bird this was.

'Is it that woodcock of yours?'

Mattis nodded stiffly.

'Yes, I heard a shot just now,' said Hege. 'And the fowler *gave* you the woodcock, then, did he?'

'No, it wasn't like that,' said Mattis. 'It wasn't his bird, was it, just because he shot it!'

'Did you take it?'

'He let me. It isn't his bird, is it? But can you *understand* it, Hege?'

To this Hege made no reply, there was really nothing she could say. They were both turned towards the bird on the table. The problem seemed to be too much for Mattis. He was becoming more and more bewildered.

'Can't you understand it?'

'No,' said Hege.

'Well, it's the same with you then,' said Mattis, bitterly. 'When things get really serious it's always like this.'

He was in a terrible state, and Hege had to think up something : 'They soon fall down of their own accord too, birds, you know. Whether or not they get shot, I mean.'

Mattis shook his head.

'They can live for years, birds, I've been told. And he looked at me too.'

'Who?'

'The bird, of course. Just as I was picking him up.'

'Was it alive?'

'I don't know, but he looked at me all right.'

'Well, we won't go on about this any more,' said Hege. 'If it wasn't alive then it didn't look at you either. It was nothing.'

All Mattis said was : 'After that he closed his eyes.'

To put an end to it Hege said firmly : 'Stop worrying about it now. Take the bird outside, I won't have it here on the table. And we're not going to use it.'

Mattis shuddered.

'Use it? No.'

'Go out and put it under a big stone, Mattis.'

'Under a big stone? Why?'

'So that nothing can run off with it, of course.'

'That's an idea,' he said gratefully.

'Then come back in as quick as you can and go to bed. Things like this can't be helped, you know. You've just got to accept them.'

'Yes, but—'

'No buts, Mattis. It's the way things are.'

'I could have said that myself,' said Mattis. 'What am I asking you for?'

Hege went into her room, shivering with cold in her thin night-dress. Mattis went outside with the woodcock and did everything just as Hege had told him.

17

By the time the difficult task had been accomplished Mattis was tired and covered in sweat. To honour the bird and to protect it he had covered it with a stone that had been far too heavy for him to lift. It felt like a really massive slab, and it had taken up all his strength. It was already midnight.

When he'd finished he sat on the stone and rested. All of a sudden he thought : If it had been Hege—

It swept through him like an icy blast in the still June night. His thoughts began to frighten him, he saw himself sitting there alone, with Hege and the bird each lying under a heavy stone.

And the eyes are closed.

And the rivers have stopped flowing.

He mumbled these words to himself, but they failed to bring him his usual sense of joy. His gaze wandered uneasily over the grassy meadow where all life seemed to be asleep. He felt cold. Come what may he had to return to Hege. Mustn't stir from her side tonight, after this.

Once more he knocked on her door.

'You must let me come in and stay with you tonight, Hege,' he said through the narrow opening. He caught a faint glimpse of his sister over by the wall under the mirror.

'Come on then,' she said, surprisingly willing.

So she wasn't asleep now either. She asked in a friendly tone as he approached : 'Did you do what I told you?'

'Yes, but—'

'Has anything else happened?' she asked quickly.

Her friendliness almost made matters worse. She ought to have been telling him off for disturbing her.

'Yes, it *has*, but I can't tell you. But that's why you've got to let me stay here with you tonight.'

'There's nothing to be frightened of,' said Hege suddenly, for no particular reason.

'Frightened? What isn't there to be frightened of?'

'I don't know, only I could hear you were frightened. You must try and forget the bird.'

'No!' he shouted. 'But I'm talking about other things as well.'

'Well come and lie down, then. I'm sure you could do with some sleep.'

He came. Lay down by Hege's side. So she smelt like a woman, even though she was his sister. His thoughts wandered far and wide.

She asked : 'Did you take off your boots?'

'Yes.'

'It was so awful about the bird,' he started again.

'It's lying safely under the stone now,' said his sister, comfortingly.

That was a strange thing to say.

'What are you talking like that for?'

Her hand brushed his cheek once or twice in answer. Nice. Made everything seem much more distant, somehow.

'Go to sleep now, Mattis.'

'That was almost like the wing of a bird,' he said referring to her fleeting hand.

Hege replied quietly : 'Yes, here we are—just as we've always been. Don't be frightened now.'

He was on the point of telling her the reason why he was lying there—but if I did, that'd be the end of your sleep tonight, Hege, he thought.

'What is it you're trying to say?' she asked, knowing him the way she did.

He gave a start.

'Nothing!'

'Well, in that case you must tell me some time in the far distant future,' said Hege, 'because we're going to stop talking now, and get some sleep.'

He longed to feel her hand, but he longed in vain.

But the dark eye.

Closed now.

And a big heavy stone over it.

Neither lid nor stone can hide an eye like that—once it has looked at you.

'Hege.'

He said it gently. She made no reply, she really seemed to be asleep—his presence had brought her peace.

Part Two

18

The clover fields were so near that their smell came wafting through the trees when the wind was in the right direction. A sure sign that it was the middle of summer.

And in an uncomfortable way Mattis became the important person in the house. Surely he was going to give a hand with the haymaking? He felt the demand hanging over him from morning till night. A grown-up lad with no job in the middle of the haymaking season—surely he can't be idling around with nothing to do?

In the cottage not a word was said about haymaking, but they had come to expect a call at this time of year, a call from someone asking Mattis to go and give a hand with the work. That was why he was the more important of them now. When you were as unsure of yourself as Mattis, this could be both pleasant and painful.

They could hear the mowing machines starting up at the crack of dawn, or clanking and clattering into the late evening. Mattis cleared his throat, that was his privilege now, for he was at the centre of things. Maybe someone would turn up.

And they went on sitting quietly.

Of course, Hege was working at top speed as always. The sweaters were taking shape.

But no call came that day. From time to time Mattis cleared his throat as if to say that he was still waiting. The following day there was no call either.

Ah well, it was no more than they expected really. Everyone knew just how much good Simple Simon was. Hege and Mattis knew, but when the mowing machines were rattling and everyone was sweating away at the hay-making you just couldn't give up waiting for a call.

'They do everything so quickly these days,' said Mattis as a kind of excuse. 'They use machines.'

Although Mattis tried to speak calmly, he was keyed up. It was a great strain to be the important person like this. Just before they went to bed, he said : 'But the wood-cock's under the stone.'

Hege stopped reluctantly.

'Well?'

'That's all. The woodcock's under the stone, whatever I do.'

'You're talking nonsense,' said Hege sharply, leaving him. At the door to her room she had already begun to regret her harsh words.

'I didn't mean it,' she said.

He was surprised. It was not often Hege took back something she'd said like that. But it gave him a chance to say to her in a light, easy tone : 'No, it's you who doesn't understand.'

She left it at that.

He wouldn't have dared to say anything like that to her last spring. He felt sure she was surprised, but she let it pass without comment.

Next morning Mattis took a stroll past the meadows where the haymaking was in progress. Not in defiance, or to show off. His reasons were a bit obscure—it was probably the sound of work that attracted him more than anything. The snorting machines. Grass tumbled, drying-racks sprang up, young and old were busy. Everyone seemed to be strong and clever. Every time he saw something beautiful, he stopped automatically.

Then he met a man coming across the road with a stack of poles over his shoulder. The man couldn't escape.

'Out for a stroll?' he had to say to Mattis.

Mattis looked at the man expectantly; the man had to say: 'If we get around to piling the hay in stacks one day soon, perhaps you could come and give us a hand when we spread them again. One morning when the weather's dry enough?'

'Yes,' said Mattis joyfully. 'I've spread haystacks before you know.'

The man strode off looking as though he'd done his good deed for the day.

Back at home Hege said that this didn't amount to anything. But Mattis felt that he'd freed himself from the demand that had been staring him in the face for almost a fortnight. Now it was Hege's turn to be the important person in the house.

Now it is night.

What can you do when everyone around you is strong and clever?

Shall never know.

But then what can you do? You have to do something, even then. All the time.

There's a streak across this house. The bird has been shot and has closed his eyes, and is covered by a stone— but the streak remains.

But what can you do?

What can you do about Hege? There's something the matter with her.

Shall never know.

But there's a gentle whisper outside now, anyway.

19

One day towards the end of July Mattis was out fishing. At least, he was out rowing in his boat. These last few weeks hadn't been at all pleasant. Well, not apart from the day he'd spent spreading hay. That day had really come, but there'd only been one of them.

Today Hege had sent him out on the lake.

He was sitting in the boat, with a far-away expression in his eyes. The lake was smooth and wide and warm. Mattis rowed a good way out from the shore, had got quite close to a rocky little island. In the far distance one or two motor-boats were humming, but apart from them the whole place was deserted. Up on land he could make out the farms he knew, and a good many others he didn't know farther down.

His fishing tackle was primitive, but the worst thing of all was the boat which let in water. Mattis sat lost in thought until the water started trickling into his shoes, then he woke up with a start, and began bailing. A moment later he was deep in thought again. His fishing rod was fastened to the stern, and the line hung limp and useless. A glaring July sun rose up from the deep, it was like being caught between two suns, sitting here in the boat. No one but Mattis went fishing on a day like this. The lake was as calm as a mill-pond.

But as far as that goes—

You catch fish when you least expect it, thought Mattis. So it isn't me who's being stupid this time.

His thoughts went back to a conversation he had had with

Hege just before he climbed into the boat: 'You think they're laughing at you when they're not doing anything of the kind.'

Yes, that's what Hege had said. It came back to him now as he sat looking at all the farms. He tried to think of someone who really wanted to hurt him and who made fun of him. But apart from children who were always a nuisance he couldn't point to a single one. They called him names behind his back, but people were like that. He found it all rather confusing.

There was a gurgling sound and water began running into his shoes. He had to start bailing hurriedly.

I mustn't think so much that I sink to the bottom, he said, bailing so fiercely that the water gushed over the side in a torrent. If I just think, the boat'll soon get full and I'll be drowned. I'd better do my thinking on dry land.

But he was soon deep in thought again, there was no stopping it. The fish weren't biting, either. He had plenty of time.

His thoughts wandered back to days and events long past. Most of them were shrouded in a kind of mist. It was his father who had been the breadwinner when he was a child. His father was like Hege, small and untiring. Clever, too. Everyone was clever except him. As far back as he could remember there'd been trouble every time he'd tried to do any work. His father had given up. His mother had gazed at him as though she would never stop hoping for a change. Then she had died, before he was fully grown up. Only a few years later his father had been killed in an accident at work. It filled Mattis with horror every time he thought of it.

After that it had been just Hege and him. Things had gone on much as they did now for many years. He had no idea when he had first been called Simple Simon—but he saw it as a grim turning point in his life.

He looked across at the shore, telling himself that no one wanted to hurt him. He thanked Hege for what she had said, and tried to hammer it in.

Then he was back bailing again. There was a quiet persistence about the water that was trying to drown him.

I want to live, I don't want to be drowned!

If only he could catch a really big fish. Come home to Hege with a really big one.

The fishes lay like thin, delicate shadows on the sandy shallows where his boat was bobbing and drifting about. They lay there idle, with nothing to do, just like Mattis himself. But terribly alert. If Mattis as much as moved his hand the fish shot off into one of the dark depths below. They weren't biting. Fishes were clever. Cleverness whichever way you turned.

And then there's Hege, he thought suddenly.

Something the matter with Hege.

He hadn't intended to let this worry him out here on the lake, but there was no escaping it : last night had been a bad night as far as Hege was concerned. That was why she'd sent him on to the lake first thing in the morning.

He had woken up at midnight, and had heard something he didn't like the sound of. It was coming from Hege's room, and he tiptoed across and peeped in. He could just see Hege lying with her face turned to the wall. He'd switched on the light, but she hadn't stirred.

Feelings of guilt had swept over him—if Hege was upset it was bound to be because of him.

'Is it me again?' he'd asked gently from over by the door.

She'd answered without turning round : 'No, it isn't you.'

'Who is it, then?'

'No one,' she'd said. 'I just don't know why I'm alive.'

As she spoke she'd turned round, fixing him with a wild stare. This was worse than he'd imagined, he was face to face with problems which went completely beyond his understanding. Hege went on: 'I get nothing out of it! Go back to your own room now, Mattis.'

As usual it was as if he were cut off by an impenetrable barrier. Hege was miserable. Something suddenly occurred to him: it was she who kept him; every single day he ate food that was bought with the money she got from her knitting.

He shook her by the shoulder: 'Hege, you've got your knitting, you know!' he'd said.

She flinched.

'Knitting? Oh! leave me alone, you don't know what you're talking about.'

And so he'd had to bring up this other matter. He'd hoped to avoid it at first, he felt so ashamed about it.

'You keep me, Hege, don't forget. You always have,' he'd said.

'It's you who keep me alive, you know,' he'd said. 'Isn't that something? Surely that's important.'

He hadn't exactly meant it like that, he just uttered the first words that came into his head.

She tried to nod her agreement, and her forehead banged against the wall with a little thud.

'I think it's important, anyway,' he'd said helplessly. 'It is for me.'

'Of course. For me too, Mattis.'

But she wasn't satisfied. She lay there turned towards the wall, refusing to show her face.

'Don't worry about this any more, Mattis. It's my own business. It'll pass, I'm sure.'

'Won't you turn round?' he'd asked.

'No,' she'd replied crossly. She wasn't going to let him see her face this time.

He stood there, his arms sagging. What could he tell her? She didn't know why she was alive. And she who was so clever. He'd shuffled back into his own room, seeing he couldn't cheer her up. It's these last few months she's got like this. What's going on?

She was back to normal again at breakfast next morning, but had asked if he couldn't take the boat out and do some fishing. He'd agreed without protest and got ready.

What's she doing back home now?

No one must see her?

He sat in the boat, deep in thought.

20

A gurgling sound came from the bottom of the boat. Quite loud this time. Mattis woke up with a start. He was halfway up to his knees in water! He must have damaged the rotten boat somewhere else today with all his trampling about—seeing the water was suddenly running in much more quickly than before.

He'd been thinking too long, that was the trouble. Hadn't noticed the water rising over his feet. The water was so warm in the summer that you didn't notice it when you were busy thinking about other things.

But this water was just as deadly dangerous as any other if you couldn't swim. He was beginning to sink, there were no two ways about it.

'No!' he shouted, his eyes wide open and staring. He

started bailing with all his might, stood knee-deep in water pushing it over the side with a broken scoop.

I'm not even forty, he thought, it's far too soon.

But his bailing wasn't doing any good, he realized, breaking out into a cold sweat. The water seemed to be rising rather than sinking. He called out in a faltering voice: 'Help! I'm sinking!'

'Someone come.'

'Come on, quickly someone!'

To no avail, far out on a wide, empty lake—and his shouts didn't carry very far either. No sound reached the farms far away in the haze. Bail as he would, the boat was getting fuller.

Things were moving quickly: a pair of eyes appeared down in the water, staring straight up at him.

'No!' he shouted.

His own eyes were staring transfixed, and the eyes in the water stared back. Nothing but a pair of eyes.

But he didn't want to.

'No, I don't want to!' he shouted, his face turning pale.

In his panic he finally caught sight of the bare, rocky island. It wasn't far away. If only he could reach it he'd be safe.

His mind was really working quickly and smoothly. He threw down the scoop, flung himself on to the seat and started struggling with the oars.

Although the boat was lying low in the water, it began to move. Mattis pulled at the oars with every ounce of strength he could muster, and more besides. He didn't stop to consider whether he had the strength or not, he had to get away from those eyes on the surface of the water.

'Hege!' he shouted wildly.

There was no chance at all of her hearing him, but still he had to shout her name. It had always been Hege he'd turned to for help.

Meanwhile the boat moved slowly towards the island. The water was rising, it was coming in through cracks higher up now. The fishing rod was bobbing up and down more forlornly than ever.

Then he stopped shouting. I'm going to make it, he thought, I'll soon be there. He pulled at the oars, full of the blissful certainty. And get there he did—before he realized it he had reached the security of the island. It was right behind him.

The boat grated against the bottom and came to rest, with the bow up on land. Mattis climbed ashore, so out of breath that he had to fling himself straight to the ground. He brought up his hand and began to wipe the sweat from his forehead.

That was a close shave. But he was safe.

He was filled with a deep sense of gratitude.

The island was nothing more than a large rock, with a few small patches of grass in the hollows. That'd be somewhere to sit, anyway. Mattis remembered to try and rescue the boat. Tried to bail it out first of all, but had to give up. He couldn't drag the waterlogged hulk far enough up on land by himself to do any good. The boat got even fuller it was so rotten, and seemed to dig itself in. The water was shallow so it didn't sink, but it remained stuck fast. Mattis sat on the shore with the end of the rope in his hand.

There was nothing for it now but to sit waiting. He was stuck here until another boat turned up. Mattis gripped the rope firmly. There was nothing to tie the boat to. Actually, it was safe enough in this calm weather, but Mattis dared not let go, a wind might spring up and set the wreck adrift—and that mustn't be allowed to happen, the boat was going to be usable again, Mattis promised himself happily.

It was blissful to relax and gradually begin thinking

again. Not that he was in any hurry about that just yet. The sun beat down upon him—no bad thing when your clothes were wringing wet; he got so hot he hadn't the energy to take them off. As yet he hadn't given a thought to getting back home; he'd saved his life, the rest would follow of its own accord.

'And a pretty mess things would have been in if I hadn't!' he said in a loud, clear voice. Out here you could talk to yourself to your heart's content.

He felt weak and tired, basking blissfully in the sun, after all the strain and excitement. Getting back on land again wouldn't be much of a problem. Sooner or later someone was bound to come out on to the lake and see him. He wasn't hungry, either, just sleepy. He could take a nap until someone turned up.

But he was afraid he might let go of the rope if he fell asleep. It was the one link between him and everything he held dear. So when he felt sleep approaching with over-powering force, he tied the boat to the only thing there was : himself. He wound the rope round one of his ankles, and made a firm knot. Admittedly the boat was resting securely on the rocks at the moment, but no one could tell how long it would stay there.

'If I look after you, then you'll look after me,' he said to the boat. Soon afterwards everything went blank.

21

Mattis didn't have any dreams this time. And when he woke up he had no idea how long he'd been asleep, he didn't even think about it, for he was awakened by rousing cries of heave-ho !

Girls' voices: 'Heave-ho!'

At the same time the rope was tightening round his ankle, and he was being pulled towards the edge of the water with violent jerks.

What on earth?

'No!' he shouted frightened and confused, sitting up and rubbing the sleep out of his eyes. And sleep vanished completely.

'Come on! Again!' came a call.

'Right! Heave-ho!'

Another jerk nearer the edge of the water. He started struggling.

'Stop it!'

Then he realized it was only a joke.

Happy laughter rolled around him. It reminded him of lovely yellow peas. A girl's voice said: 'You'd better get up chum, or you'll end up in the water.'

Another girl said: 'Wouldn't it be a good idea to bail out your boat? It's stuck on the bottom.'

Mattis shook his head to free himself of the suspicion that he was seeing things. Then he banged his left hand hard against the rock—it was so painful that he groaned. His heart was pounding with excitement. He wasn't dreaming, yet here he was, in the company of friendly, smiling girls.

'Shall we untie you from the boat?' they asked full of laughter. 'You look so silly.'

'I'm sure I do,' he answered without thinking, still trying to clear his head.

'And there's nothing new or unusual about that either,' he said waking up even more, his eyes opening even wider.

They didn't listen to what he was saying. Didn't understand what he was talking about. One of them bent over him and undid the rope round his foot. Mattis looked at her shyly, felt her hands touch his naked foot—the whole thing was unbelievable, almost too good to be true. At last he managed to take in the whole scene. The boat the girls had arrived in lay splendid and newly varnished, pulled up next to his own sunken wreck—and here stood two happy young girls, obviously on holiday by the look of their sun-tanned bodies. There were a couple of faded anoraks or whatever they were lying in the boat, the girls were wearing nothing but their bathing costumes, ready to plunge head first into the water.

Mattis looked at them quickly. He mustn't do anything stupid now. If he spoilt this, it would take him a long, long time to get over it.

'It's almost as if my dreams and wishes were coming true,' he said to begin with, looking across at the distant shores. He mustn't stare at *them*.

'I *have* dreamt quite a few things as a matter of fact,' he finished off unexpectedly.

The girls looked at him, surprised.

'Really?'

'Yes, but don't ask me any more about it,' he said. 'I haven't told anybody.'

'No, all right,' said one of the girls, 'we have dreams ourselves, so we know what they're like.'

And they gave him a friendly glance.

They're clever, too, he thought.

'But I've seen plenty like you!' he said, once again unexpectedly. Had to be tough. 'There are crowds of them on the road here in the summer!' he said, 'in the store and everywhere. You mustn't think—'

He stopped. Just stared at them defiantly. It was all right to look at them, he felt, as long as it was an angry, defiant look.

They were smiling, as friendly as ever.

'Oh, we know that all right,' they said. 'Didn't think for a moment that you were just anybody.'

Mattis looked at them quickly, deeply grateful that they knew nothing about him. Surprised, too, at the way he'd spoken out. Without hesitation he'd let them have it, and looked them straight in the eye.

But now he turned away again, and asked quietly, in a different tone : 'Where on earth have you come from?'

They pointed unconcernedly down over the hazy blue shores where Mattis was a stranger.

'We've been staying down there for a fortnight.'

'As the weather was so nice today we thought we'd take a longish trip in the rowing boat,' said one of them.

'And then we made for this little island to bathe,' said the other winking at him, 'but as we drew closer we saw something rather odd.'

You mustn't, said a voice inside him every time he wanted to turn round and look at them. He was still staring fixedly down towards the unknown shores. Meanwhile they went on with their story.

'At first we thought there'd been an accident, but when we got closer, we saw there was nothing to worry about.'

'Yes, it'd have been an odd sort of accident,' said Mattis, breaking into her story. He felt so happy it hurt.

'Well, there must have been an accident of some kind,' one of the girls said. 'It looks as if you only just managed to reach the island in safety.'

Mattis snorted.

'Nothing to worry about. Not now *you're* here,' he added with real feeling.

'How very nicely put,' they said.

Those were words he would treasure. They thought it was well put. Clever perhaps.

'Have you seen me before?' he asked, trembling inwardly, but it had to be faced. 'I mean on the road or in the store or anywhere else?'

They shook their heads. A blissful sight.

'We live a long way off, you see, so we don't really know anyone round here.'

'Not heard about me either?'

'How can we tell, if we don't know who you are?'

Razor-sharp, he thought. That's the sort of answer some people can give.

Although he was looking across at the distant shores, he still managed to get a glimpse of the girls from the side. Saw them shaking their heads. They didn't know a thing. Wonderful.

'I'm glad to hear that,' he said—but was quite incapable of saying how desperately glad he was.

The girls turned it into a joke: 'Have you got such a bad reputation then?'

Pooh! What did it matter to him if they joked about it. What he'd been asking about on the other hand seemed like a matter of life and death at this moment.

'What are you looking at out there on the lake all the time?' they asked him.

'Nobody. Nothing at all,' he answered quickly.

'There must be something.'

'It's not that,' he said seriously, 'but I'm sorely tempted.'

All the smiles seemed to have vanished, all the winks, too, the girls grew quite quiet. It was the way Mattis looked. One of them said gently: 'Are you afraid to look at us?'

'I'm very tempted to,' he answered in a low voice, without moving.

She didn't go on. Mattis's heart lay exposed and defenceless. The two friends looked at each other bewildered. His voice, his face, his eyes, all drove anything resembling a giggle out of their minds. They were confused, and they were disturbed.

'We can go away again if you like,' said one of them

embarrassed, 'row over to the shore and fetch some people to come and give you a hand with your boat.'

'No, no!' he shouted, holding them back.

The other girl found a solution: 'Come on, Anna, let's go and bathe like we said. It's just right here now.'

'Yes, let's,' answered the girl called Anna. She seemed to be relieved. 'That'd be marvellous.'

'Cheerio for now!' they called over their shoulders to Mattis.

Then they dived into the warm summer water. Propelled themselves forward with the free and easy movement of two fishes, moved away. Mattis watched them to his heart's content

And they'll have to come back,, he thought, trembling with joy. They'll have to fetch their boat. They'll have to come back on to the island.

'I hardly dare think,' he said in a low voice as he watched them swimming away from him. They were chattering busily out there. Before long they stopped and waved to him.

'Hello!'

Mattis didn't move. But then he lifted up his hand with a stiff, jerky movement, and lowered it again, shyly.

They were coming back towards him now in a whirl of water, high-spirited and confident once more.

'You must let us bring you back to land and save your life!' they shouted to him—treading water and splashing about, and thrusting their toes into the air.

'It's a long way!' he shouted back at once, frightened. At the same time their words sent a feeling of excitement and joy running through him again.

'We've got the whole day before us,' they answered, bubbles and splutters coming from their red lips. 'If you'll tell us your name we'll row you back to land, and we'll put you ashore as gently as if you'd been made of glass.'

He shook his head. But they weren't going to give up. They were having great fun, swimming round the island calling out to him and talking about themselves.

'My name's Anna, and that's Inger. It's as simple as that. And now it's your turn.'

He shook his head.

'No! I've said no.'

'All right then, you can jolly well stay there till you change your mind, you obstinate donkey,' they said and went on splashing about.

'You don't know anything!' he shouted to them. 'Shut up! d'you hear! There's no need to say things like that.'

They didn't understand him, turned away, splashing, diving and playing about.

They mustn't leave me, he thought. They mustn't! It's only just this once. But then he bent his head and took it all back: It'd probably be better if they went with things as they are now. They don't know anything about me yet.

They came out of the water gasping for breath, tossed their hair back, got some towels out of the boat and dried themselves and lay down to sunbathe right next to where Mattis was sitting—the island was so small they had no choice.

'You'll have to excuse us,' said Inger, 'but there isn't exactly room to hide on this island, and there are sharp rocks everywhere except here. You'll have to put up with us.'

Then both the girls dozed off. The sun shone down on them. Mattis breathed in the sweet smell that rose up.

Inside Mattis storms were raging. He couldn't move. Couldn't jump into his boat, because it lay on the bottom full of water. He searched desperately for another boat he could wave to. There was none.

Thank God, said a voice inside him.

Bewildered as he was he knew that he wouldn't have

missed this for anything. They didn't realize who he was, he could sit here and be someone else. On the strength of this he succumbed to the temptation and looked at them openly as they lay there dozing.

What was it?

Strange, that was all. Unbelievable.

Can't last, either.

Smelling a sweet smell I've always known about.

Actually seeing this.

Soon afterwards he gave a start: saw Anna looking at him out of the corner of her eye—the eye nearest to him was peeping out through a crack. He turned away as if he'd been stung.

I've never been so tempted before. What'll Hege say now?

The storm raged in him unabated. No one moved. The naked bodies gave off their sweet smell.

After a while Mattis spoke, and a shudder ran down his spine: 'Per,' he said. It wasn't directed to anyone in particular.

Anna opened her eyes wide, and raised herself up a little, right next to him.

'What did you say?'

'Per.'

It was awful, but he did it, couldn't resist it any longer.

Inger was quicker than Anna, it seemed. She sat up a little. Knew straight away what Mattis was talking about.

'So his name's Per. He's told us after all then, like we insisted.'

A smile spread across Anna's face.

'Of course! Hello there Per. Nice of you to tell us at long last.'

Mattis nodded, horrified at himself.

'Now we'll row you ashore. A promise is a promise.

But let's stay here and enjoy ourselves a bit longer first, eh Per?' said Anna.

'Yes, of course,' Inger answered for him. It was frightening the way Inger saw into his mind and could guess his wishes. Mattis felt as if he were walking on air.

'Just think, if Hege—' he began, and stopped short. 'Nothing!' he said.

But they'd heard all right.

'Who's Hege? Your girl-friend?'

'My girl-friend? No, my sister. But it's not like—' and he stopped short again.

'Nothing at all, d'you hear! Things get along perfectly all right at home, as long as you're really sharp-witted, and Hege is.'

'I'm sure she is,' said Inger.

'Heavens, yes! If only one was really sharp-witted the whole time,' said Anna, 'things'd be easy then.'

'Yes, so you felt like a newly sharpened knife,' said Mattis, playing with dangerous words.

'Ugh yes!' they both replied together.

Be careful now, Mattis, a warning voice in the background seemed to be murmuring. A rather insistent murmur too—but this would never happen again. I mustn't behave like this, deceiving people. I know I mustn't. But it's only this once.

'What's done can't be undone,' he said in a loud and serious voice. Continuing his train of thought.

'Yes, that's rather a sharp-witted remark, too,' said Inger patiently.

Was this happiness? Happiness had come to him on a bare, rocky island, without any kind of warning. He hadn't done anything to bring it about. He could even make sharp-witted remarks.

There lay the two girls, weren't a bit afraid of him.

they were so near, he could have put out his hand and touched them. The sun was turning them a golden brown for him, had been shining on them for fourteen days.

He had to do something. And it had to be something out of the ordinary.

'Anna and Inger,' he said in a soft voice. Said both their names for the first time.

They raised themselves up on their elbows, compelled by the earnestness of his voice and the gleam in his eyes.

'Yes? We're listening,' they said, expectantly.

If anyone had ever spoken their names with affection, it was now. They answered straight away, humbly : yes, we're listening. This was no ordinary moment.

And Mattis was complete master of the situation. Sat looking at the two girls. He spoke gently, to avoid upsetting anything.

'That was all.'

With those words everything seemed to have been said. The girls, too, seemed to feel he'd said the thing they were longing most of all to hear. He'd put it in a form they accepted.

'Per,' they said in return. Looked up into his helpless face, which had suddenly become transformed. Despite its miserable and awkward appearance there was something in it that was beautiful beyond all description. None of them stirred.

It couldn't last. Mattis knew it couldn't. The storm that was threatening in the background began to catch up with him. He must be tough and tear himself away.

'Anna and Inger,' he said in a new tone of voice which made them feel uneasy.

'What is it?' asked Anna, a little frightened.

'Just as we were lying here so comfortably,' said Inger, 'can't we carry on?'

Anna looked around her: the lake, the shores, the blue haze, the ridges—her own fragrant body was no doubt included as well. Suddenly she turned to Mattis, full of it all: 'If this isn't a paradise you're living in, then I don't know what is,' she said, nervous under his staring gaze.

'It's not so easy living here,' Mattis blurted out.

'What do you mean?'

'You don't know anything!' he said. 'You're sitting here thinking something different from what *I'm* thinking.'

A frowning expression came over their faces.

'About what?'

'Do you notice anything peculiar about me?' he asked. He couldn't leave the subject alone.

Anna said firmly and decisively: 'We don't want to know anything more than what we know already Per, so please stop it!'

And Inger said: 'Yes. Please stop it!'

This shut him up, and not only him: it put an end to the murmuring in the background as well. He didn't need to be tough with himself any longer. What wonderful girls these were.

'Well, that's all right then,' he answered. 'If you don't say anything, nothing's said.'

He thought that must have been a rather sharp-witted remark.

They nodded, too.

Then they started laughing—freed from something which had been awkward and embarrassing, yet moving as well. They dabbled their toes in the water.

'We're very glad you were here on the island today,' said Inger.

Mattis looked at Anna, expectantly.

'Me too,' said Anna quickly.

'Me too,' said Mattis, quite unconcernedly.

'And now we'll row you home, like the kind girls we

are,' they said to him, and got up almost blinding him again.

22

Anna and Inger pushed their boat into the water. It lay there bobbing up and down, strong and sturdy, only just touching the surface, it was so light when it was empty.

'Come on, Per.'

'But what about this?' said Mattis, pointing to his own waterlogged wreck. 'I must take it with me, or I'll never get out on the lake again.'

'But how can we manage?'

Mattis knew how. On this occasion he was quite confident.

'I'll take command,' he said. 'But you must do exactly what I tell you.'

He stood full of gratitude for what had happened. He told the girls to get into the water and then they'd all rock the boat backwards and forwards so that the water would splash over the side. They managed to do it just the way he wanted, got some of the water out so the little boat began to float. Then he got them to rock the boat by themselves while he tugged at the mooring rope.

They struggled and rocked and pulled—and in the end they got the boat half-way out of the water.

The girls liked this heavy work, they laughed and laughed, went and fetched a decent scoop and bailed the boat properly. There was a hole a little way up on one side, but Mattis thought of something at once, pulled off one of his socks and stood poking bits of it into the hole with his knife.

114

"That'll do as long as there's nobody in it,' he said, 'this place'll be above the water then.'

He felt quite dizzy busying himself with all this right under their eyes, and succeeding as well.

And Anna said too : 'We can see you know all about boats.'

Mattis laughed proudly.

'Just wait a bit,' he said.

He had a great secret he was soon going to tell them : he was an expert rower, too. And he was going to insist on having the oars.

His own boat was tied to the girls' by the mooring rope. Inger was already sitting down and taking hold of the oars in her accustomed way.

'Oh no you don't !' said Mattis. 'It's me who's going to do the rowing, of course.'

'Is it?'

What a moment this was.

'Yes, maybe I know even more about rowing !'

'Well, of course, then, you'd obviously better row. And besides you're a man.'

'That's true,' he said.

'And I know a lot about stopping up holes,' he added.

'Yes, there's no doubt you'll have to give way, Inger,' said Anna.

Inger sat down beside Anna in the back of the boat. Mattis, as the master, took up the oars.

'I didn't want to tell you about this really,' he said to the girls. He felt so sure of himself at this moment a fresh fib didn't really matter.

'About what?'

'The rowing, of course.'

Mattis was bubbling over with confidence. He'd never been so glad about being able to row before. He even felt he could match himself against the clever ones, if need be. He set off with long, steady strokes.

'Nice piece of work,' he said.

'Our boat?'

'Yes, of course.'

'What else?' he asked when he'd had time to think it over.

They laughed, relieved and happy.

'No, nothing else, of course not.'

'Well, you can land wherever you like,' said Inger. 'We're in no particular hurry, all we've got to do is get back home in time for supper, and we're only lazing about here anyway.'

'I've set my course,' Mattis replied curtly.

This was how it should be. This was what he ought to have been able to say about so many things: I know all about this. And: I've set my course. And much more. His strokes slackened and became uneven.

'Hey, wake up!' they shouted at him.

He gave a start. The girls looked inclined to tease him.

'You almost fell asleep, Per.'

'Oh blast!' he said, stifling his dream.

The boat in tow came bobbing and bouncing behind them, got along quite well as long as there was nobody in it.

Mattis looked at the girls. They could have little idea of what they'd done for him today.

'Anna and Inger,' he said, from the bottom of his heart.

They looked at him expectantly. It was the tone of his voice. But he said no more.

'Now make sure you row in a dead straight line after all that boasting,' they said, playing with their toes in the bottom of the boat. They somehow felt that this strange person had managed to thank them for something, and their sense of joy went right down to their toes.

'I always row dead straight, it's the only thing I can do,' Mattis blurted out, and gave a start—but fortunately they didn't seem to have heard this last careless remark.

'Right-oh then,' they said.

At first Mattis steered straight for home. Then he thought of a better plan: he'd row *where there were people*. He wanted to be seen with the girls, this was an opportunity not to be missed. He'd put in at the old pier by the store, where there were lots of houses all around. There was bound to be someone walking past who'd see this unusual landing.

I'll arrive like a prince, he thought. All who wish may come and watch.

'We'll row up to the pier by the store where I do my shopping first,' he announced, 'there are bound to be people there who'll see us.'

'People who'll see us? What's the point of that?' they asked together.

He didn't understand.

'Don't tell me you're conceited, Per?' asked Inger, letting her forefinger trail lazily in the water as they rowed along.

'Conceited?' he said mystified.

He saw Anna make a sign to Inger. Inger said quickly: 'Of course we'll land wherever it suits you best, not another word about it.'

Behind Mattis the wake of the boat lay as straight as a die. Now it swung round abruptly as he changed course for the pier and people. Above him the day towered like a great arch.

Hege won't believe a word of this when I get home. I ought really to have rowed them there as well. But arriving at the pier like this is top of the list, all the same.

'The very top of the list,' he said in a loud voice, deliberately making it sound meaningless.

'What do you mean, Per?'

'Today, of course! Day of all days.'

Things were working properly inside his head.

'Very nicely put,' they said. They kept on praising him for the things he said.

Inger said: 'We shall remember today, too, Per.'

But her words cast a shadow over Mattis. Remember. They were going to go away, were going to remember this meeting somewhere else, in a strange place, without him. That must never be!

The girls had begun to pay close attention to him by now, and Anna asked at once: 'Anything wrong?'

He gave a mighty pull at the oars, and then another. Inger realized at once what she ought to say.

'Surely you can see there's nothing the matter with *him*, Anna.'

She's the really clever one, Mattis thought, and gazed enraptured at Inger.

Yes, he was looking straight at them now—even though they were almost naked. The shyness he had felt on the island had vanished, they were like old friends now.

'Anna and Inger,' he said from where he sat.

They waited.

Nothing more. It was enough.

The pier and the houses were rapidly drawing nearer. Mattis increased the speed still more. It was a difficult choice: if he rowed slowly, this wonderful moment would last even longer—if he rowed at top speed, the girls would be gone sooner, but they'd remember what a great rower he was. He chose the latter, all things considered.

'Gosh! are we going to go even faster, Per?' the girls asked delighted.

He'd made the right choice.

'We can never go too fast,' said Mattis, 'but you wouldn't understand that. Now have a look, as you're facing that way, and see if you can spot anyone on the pier, or on the road near by.'

'Don't see anybody, but then we're too far away.'

Anna saw something : 'There goes a car.'

'Cars don't count,' said Mattis, 'they just rush past without seeing anything.'

After a little while Anna said, from her look-out post :

'There's a man standing on the pier now—but I can't see which way he's facing.'

Inger added : 'Someone's just come out of the store, Per. It looks as though there's going to be a reception.'

'Now they've gone, Per, both of them.'

Mattis was being peppered with information. He heaved and strained at the oars, more than was good for him. But he had to make this landing look impressive, whatever the cost. Never again in his whole life would he have the chance of arriving in such style, with two radiant girls sitting in the boat.

'People have seen us now,' said Anna. 'There are a couple of boys standing staring at us. We can see things better now, how big they are, and which way people are facing and everything.'

'Oh, boys,' said Mattis coldly, 'we don't want too many of them.'

'Someone on a bike has just stopped.'

'No, he's going into the store.'

'Oh well. Still, things have started happening,' said Mattis earnestly. He was beginning to feel very tired, and his arms were numb. Fast rowing like this was not his forte, but he wasn't going to give in now. He gave a quick glance over his shoulder, saw a number of people on the pier. And then he directed all his attention to keeping the wake dead straight to the very last.

More people had stopped and were beginning to congregate on the pier now—when they saw it was Simple

Simon, but a Simple Simon quite unlike the one they knew. And it was a landing worth stopping for: like some triumphant victor from distant shores the shining boat came gliding in in the glittering sun, and in the back sat two sun-tanned girls, waving with lazy, friendly gestures in the direction of the pier. And Mattis was in command, knew everything about rowing, steered safely and securely, anything but a simpleton.

Everything was going off perfectly, down to the very last detail.

Mattis's own boat was still in tow, but it had taken in some water, which made the going heavier. All the same, Mattis managed to keep his speed up until he was forced to turn to avoid the supports under the pier. No one watching realized how close he had come to exhaustion—but anyway, his strength was returning now, in the sheer excitement and joy of it all.

There was quite a little crowd waiting on the pier to receive them. Five or six, at least. And how many those six could tell the story to afterwards! That was the point. Six times six times six times six, at least.

Mattis had had time to consider how he was going to round the whole thing off, and now the moment had arrived. As the boat glided in towards the edge of the pier, the master rose with dignity from his seat and laid down the oars on either side of him.

'Well, you'll have to take over yourselves now, girls,' he said quietly, but loud enough for everybody to hear. 'We've reached land.'

'They can see that for themselves, I should think,' came the glib rejoinder from a boy. But he was silenced at once by a voice from the crowd.

'Oh shut up!'

'Now I just want my own boat back,' Mattis continued, turned towards the girls.

There was a radiant smile on the girls' faces.

The little crowd on land stood spellbound, not daring to move. For one thing there were the two self-confident girls, but it wasn't just that—Simple Simon himself had managed everything without a hitch, and with such ease that they hardy recognized him. The boy had another try though, in his whining voice, standing looking down into Mattis's wreck of a boat: 'Been on the bottom, Mattis?'

Mattis didn't seem to hear him. Calmly he untied his boat from the new one. Then he turned to the girls once more: 'Anna and Inger,' he said, in the special way their names had to be spoken.

They looked up at him, standing where he was on the edge of the pier, trying to control his emotions.

'Thanks for the trip,' he said, in the midst of all the people. It was an entirely new experience for him to be standing like this, saying things like this, to people like this.

The golden girls, Anna and Inger, said: 'Thank *you*, Per. We'll never forget this.'

I think I'd like to die now, he suddenly thought. But he checked himself. No, on second thoughts, then I wouldn't be able to enjoy it any longer.

The boy shrilled: 'Per? He's not called Per at all. This is Mattis.'

It felt like a stab in the back—but if only it stopped there. If only the boy didn't blurt out the whole truth: this is Simple Simon. That's what we call him. Oh God, they mustn't say it.

He counted the seconds.

And he was spared. It must have been Anna and Inger that did it, he thought. They were standing up in the boat now, young and glorious, and so obviously on his side, gazing coldly at the boy every time he opened his mouth.

'Mattis or Per, it's all the same to us,' they said proudly, putting the wretched youth in his place and shutting him up.

They made round, swinging movements with their arms: 'Cheerio then, Per, and thanks. We'll be off home now, too. Perhaps we'll meet again some day.'

The girls moved off. Mattis stood swallowing. But he held his head up. Then he had to go and tie his old hulk to an iron hook.

The five or six people who were standing there didn't ask any questions, something had taken hold of them. They were embarrassed somehow. One of them even said to Mattis: 'They're waving to you.'

Mattis straightened up quickly and waved back. The boat was rapidly growing smaller. The girls, too, were good at rowing, but of course it was easier now.

Then someone in the crowd plucked up courage: 'Well, you've got yourself involved in something all right, Mattis.'

Mattis didn't flinch.

'Yes, I have,' he said.

The boy came to life again: 'Going to take them for any more trips, then?'

'Maybe,' Mattis replied calmly.

He believed it. No sooner had he said it than it was true. Why shouldn't it happen again?

'We've been up to all sorts of things today,' he added, looking straight at the boy.

Someone laughed, but it wasn't an unpleasant laugh. At least, it didn't seem like that to Mattis. He'd finished here, and could walk away. The people on the pier were his friends, they'd been kind and hadn't exposed him. He didn't really *walk*, though, it was more as though he was being borne home to Hege on wings. On the way he kept an eye on the lake: the boat itself was growing smaller and smaller.

23

The excitement had subsided a little by the time he got home. Just about right, he'd be able to tell the whole story in an orderly manner. The happy boat had disappeared behind blue headlands—Mattis realized it was gone for good. The girls would be leaving, and he wasn't likely ever to meet them again.

But all the same, the event was undeniably true and great. There was no need to add a single little lie to what he was going to tell his sister, the truth itself was more than enough. Hege seemed to be busier than usual with her knitting as she listened to him, giving only the occasional murmured reply.

'You're listening, aren't you?' he asked, 'because things like this only happen once in a lifetime you know.'

'Of course,' she replied, 'I've heard every word, I could repeat the whole lot.'

The sad significance of only once and never again was lost on him for the moment. He was still using it to cast a golden glow over the event.

He went on with his story. An incredible number of things had happened to him and the two girls. Hege listened with a contented expression on her face. Mattis was a bit irritated by the fact that she went on knitting just the same as ever. She never knitted on Sundays—and surely this was as important as a Sunday. In the end he said : 'Can't you put that sweater down for a bit?'

'What for?'

'It's sort of like Sunday, for me.'

She let the sweater fall into her lap and concentrated

on listening. He had reached a crucial point. Full of gratitude he told her about Anna and Inger's words of farewell.

'We'll never forget this,' they said. 'Per or Mattis, it's all the same to us,' they said.

No, Anna and Inger didn't come up to his end of the lake again. But Mattis lived in a rather different world from before. He felt more confident, walked down the road with more confidence, entered the store in a different way. Everyone knew what had happened, you could tell that by looking at them. The first six had done their job properly, everything else followed of its own accord.

This was the way things went in the store now: the storekeeper weighed the little packet of coffee, and asked casually, while keeping an eye on the scales: 'Been out rowing again?'

'No.'

Mattis's answer was brief and casual, too, but inwardly he was laughing. This was the way to talk about great events. Admittedly this very same storekeeper had been making remarks behind his back recently, but you just had to ignore that. He also took great care not to buy any sweets on these first visits—what were camphor drops now? He walked out through the door with his coffee and sugar, like a lumberjack from the wild forests.

Then he heard that Anna and Inger had really left—he met people from the place where they'd been staying, and plucked up courage and asked. Their holidays were over.

24

In place of the girls came the storm which so far that summer had been kind enough to keep out of the way. It had to come sooner or later. It came the fourth day after the adventure on the lake. The fourth morning.

Mattis noticed it the moment he got out of the house: the heavy, oppressive atmosphere couldn't be lightly dismissed. The sky was dark and motionless. Of course clouds like that might not mean anything more than rain, and yet. . . . Mattis had the same leaden feeling in his own body, and when that happened he knew what was in store. All the energy seemed to seep out of him. In the meantime he watched the expression on Hege's face.

Hege went on as though there was nothing the matter.

'Don't you see!' he exclaimed at last.

'I can't see anything unusual,' she replied, and went on tidying up the house. 'What is it that you see, then?'

'The thunderstorm.'

'Oh, is that all,' she said.

Mattis drifted aimlessly in and out of the house. During all the years he had been frightened of thunderstorms he had learned to recognize many strange signs which he used today to size up the situation. The most reliable one was the leaden feeling around and inside him.

Hege said comfortingly: 'Won't come to anything, you know. It'll soon clear up again, this thunderstorm of yours.'

'You can't fool me like that today,' he said. 'I don't think I've ever seen it looking quite so black before.'

No sooner had he spoken than there was a faint rumble

of thunder. Thunder still in its sleep, but just as threatening, none the less. Mattis went hot all over.

'Did you hear that?'

'Yes, I heard it, but that may be the end of it. Try and calm down now,' said Hege. 'Stay *here* for a bit this time, it's just as safe, you see if it isn't.'

'It's coming as sure as you're standing there washing up the cups. Listen!'

The thunder rumbled again, a little louder this time—the way it always is.

'Still, wait a bit though,' said Hege.

'Why don't you come with me instead?' said Mattis, more and more nervous.

'Certainly not. Now wait.'

In this situation Mattis was deaf to all pleas and good advice. His face had turned grey, he was already off to his shelter, the one he always used during thunderstorms. The privy was the safest place. Over the years Mattis had collected a large number of stories about lightning and what it did—but it had never struck a privy. Strange, but true.

The third rumble came before he could get inside—much nearer this time. Apart from that there was an uncanny silence. Not a bird sang. The only sound he could hear was the buzzing of a bluebottle which flashed past him in a blur of blue through the electrified air.

He closed the door securely.

He didn't have long to wait before the storm broke with a vengeance. Outside the lightning flashed with a soft and dangerous hiss, and Mattis sat huddled up, his eyes closed, counting one, two, three until the crash came. He dug his fingers into his ears twisting and turning them and producing an awful noise, but it wasn't much help when the thunder really got going.

'Heavens! Listen to *that*—'

Wilder still.

And Hege in the midst of it all.

What's she doing now? Sitting knitting sweaters in weather like this, too? With the lightning hissing all around? No, she can't be. She must have that much sense.

The storm was raging. So far the rain had held off. Mattis was in the first and worst part of the thunderstorm, the rainless part. And who knows, perhaps the old rules are changed today—maybe this place isn't safe any longer.

Because that day's bound to come sooner or later, I suppose. Everything comes sooner or later really.

Not safe here either.

He wriggled his fingers furiously round in his ears. Flash and thunderclap were coming together now. Well, let it come then, he said to himself, numb with fear. One, two, three. It wasn't the interval between lightning and thunder he was counting, it was the time he had left to live. The ground seemed to give, at least once. The rain was coming down in buckets now. I think I get more and more frightened each time, but then it gets more and more dangerous each time.

Hege's sitting in the kitchen and isn't a bit frightened. Isn't frightened of anything.

It turned out to be a long struggle. The rain hammered down on the roof. The water was coming through in drips and trickles as well—the roof was in a poor state, like everything else here.

But it had to come to an end. At least the worst part of the storm was over now, and that was an immense relief.

So today wasn't going to be an exception from the rule either.

The shelter had proved safe. His body began to relax, now he felt easier in his mind. There were still one or two faint, harmless rumbles to be heard, and the rain was teeming down. It was wonderful to have the storm behind you. Soon he'd be rushing through the last of it and in to Hege.

Now!

He flung open the door and dashed headlong through the rain. There was a strong smell of wet leaves and grass. A smell you never got except at moments like this.

Through flashing fire, he thought as he stood on the doorstep shaking the water off himself. He didn't doubt for a moment that Hege would be sitting quietly in the kitchen. A thunderstorm had never made Hege run away.

And sure enough, there was his sister, getting on with her work. At least she was now.

'Have you been sitting like that all the time?'

'Oh there you are,' she said, not answering his question.

'Through flashing fire,' he said, and all of a sudden his rainsoaked face broke into a proud and confident smile.

25

After this Mattis set off to explore as he usually did after a storm. His body felt fresh and restored. White streams were foaming down the hillsides. But Mattis didn't get very far this time, he stopped suddenly, riveted to the spot: What does that mean!

It was the aspens, Mattis-and-Hege, only one of them now rose up to its full height. The other had been shattered by the lightning, all that could be seen was a bit of white trunk low down. There hadn't been a fire, the rain must have put it out at once.

Death had been at work over there.

Mattis stood there without moving for a long time.

This was—well it was a kind of omen! But which of them was it meant for? Which was Mattis and which was Hege?

At first he wanted to call Hege, but he stopped himself. Perhaps she knew *which was which*—and in that case he dare not talk about it openly to her. But he had to find out who it was meant for, he must try and be crafty.

Quietly he returned to Hege: 'Did you really sit knitting?'

'Yes,' she replied. It was obvious what he was referring to.

'Things might have gone really badly.'

'Oh?'

'Lightning has struck just the other side of the fence,' he said stiffly, as though pronouncing a verdict.

'Really,' said Hege. 'Yes, there was one clap of thunder that was much worse than the others.'

'It's shattered a tree-top.'

'Uh-huh,' said Hege, counting stitches.

'One of the withered aspens!'

She didn't bat an eyelid.

'Oh, really?' she said.

'Well, if that isn't important either,' he said angrily, 'then nothing's important, I can tell you.'

'Lightning's attracted to withered tree-tops,' said Hege. She said it without a thought. Straight out.

'Go and see if you can spot any more that have been struck, Mattis,' she went on.

'Right-oh,' he replied in an eager voice—for this was a straightforward task that he could cope with.

When he got outside he began scrutinizing the tree-tops. After a while he realized that Hege had fooled him. She didn't want to hear about the aspen that had been struck, so she thought up this idea of counting tree-tops. But why didn't she?

He went back in and reported: 'No more.'

'Good,' said Hege. Just like that.

But the fact that the aspen had been struck by lightning made Mattis feel uneasy. He wandered in and out of the house and up and down the road. But he found no solution to the problem.

It's a question of life and death, he thought all of a sudden.

Who's been hit?

He couldn't get anything more out of Hege, she refused to tell what she knew. He had no choice but to turn to strangers—but the mere thought of it filled him with dread. And he would have to be sharp-witted as well. But it's a question of life and death. If it isn't Hege, it's me.

Which would you rather? said a voice inside him.

Mustn't think like that! he said to himself, bringing his thoughts to an abrupt halt. I've stopped thinking about it.

He would have to pretend he wanted to make a trip to the store, he made trips there more often now. Since his great moment on the pier recently he walked calmly into the store in front of everybody in a way he'd never done before. For all he knew he was a respected man now—rowing up with the girls like that had really been a tremendous success.

So one afternoon he asked : 'Do you want me to go and do any shopping today?' He had even shaved.

'You're a changed person these days,' said Hege. 'Always pestering me about going to the store.'

He didn't protest. She had no idea what the real reason for his trip was, that it was a matter of life and death.

'But what about money?' he said, feeling rather small.

She found some money for the shopping, and a little bit extra for Mattis.

'That's for—'

'I don't want any sweets this time,' he said quickly, 'if that's what you're thinking.'

'Why not? We're no worse off now than we've been before.'

'But how can you think about sweets when lightning shatters the tree-tops,' said Mattis and succeeded in touching briefly on the secret topic. But it had no effect on Hege.

'I don't see why you shouldn't,' Hege said, frightening him with her frivolity.

'Surely there are more important things to think about now? I thought you'd understood that, too.'

'Take the money, Mattis,' said Hege unmoved. 'Buy yourself some sweets the same as you've always done.'

'Be careful!' said Mattis, in great agitation. And he left the extra money behind on the table so that he had just enough with him to pay for the serious items. He had to get away before she frightened him even more.

What he wanted was a good excuse for walking along the main road, and perhaps meeting some of his nearest neighbours—they were bound to know more about the two tree-tops than anyone else. The storekeeper lived a little too far away to know which was which. Mattis had to find out who had been hit.

There were no local people on the road at this time of the day, everyone was at work. Mattis had forgotten about that. Cars went swishing past him. He went to the store and did his shopping, calmly and with authority. As usual there were a couple of strangers there, holidaymakers buying biscuits and lemonade.

As Mattis was about to leave, something embarrassing happened. Since he hadn't bought his usual little bag of sweets the storekeeper must have thought he hadn't got enough money—so he quickly dug out a few camphor drops and made a paper cone. He put the cone next to the other things Mattis had bought, giving him a little wink.

Mattis blushed. He had seen the storekeeper doing the same sort of thing with children. Quickly he snatched up the two or three bags he had bought, and left the sweets lying on the counter.

'Take that one as well,' said the storekeeper. 'You can pay for them some other time.'

These words put Mattis in an embarrassing spot. He was being given sweets like a child—although he knew about great things like shattered trees and lightning and omens of death. He took the gift, mumbling a thank you, and even popped a sweet into his mouth. Had been made to feel small. The worst of it was that the storekeeper had only been trying to be kind. Mattis had to try and save face.

'Well, I suppose you can't really help it,' he said in a loud voice to the storekeeper.

That was better. The storekeeper stared at him a little: 'What can't I help?'

'Being like you are, of course!' Mattis replied, feeling he had managed the whole thing rather well.

The other man laughed contentedly, felt he was on safe ground again.

'Well no, I hope not.'

Mattis left.

Once outside he couldn't resist taking another sweet. He placed one on each side of his mouth and let the strong, sweet flavour ooze on to his tongue—it seemed such a long time since he'd last done this.

The whole time he encountered nothing but strangers on the road. He wandered about, staring emptily at the cars rushing past him, and keeping close to the withered tree-tops where they were visible from the road. But the afternoon came to an end at last, and people began to leave the fields and return home. Those who were working for other farmers had come on to the road, several of them. There was a man coming along now, and Mattis headed straight for him with an exploratory question : 'Well, what have you been doing today?'

It was ill chosen. The man was tired and gave Mattis an irritated glance.

'What have *you* been doing today?' he countered, and wanted to be on his way.

Mattis gave a start. But he mustn't let himself be frightened now.

'It's something important,' he said firmly. 'I only asked that other question because it's the sort of thing people do.

The man must have realized who he was talking to by now; when he spoke his tone was kinder.

'I've been haymaking, there are still quite a few who haven't finished yet,' he said. And he plonked himself down on a lop-sided guard-stone at the side of the road.

'Now tell me what it's all about, Mattis, quickly. I'm tired and hungry.'

'I don't know *how* to say it,' said Mattis terrified. 'I can't do it quickly!'

'Then perhaps we could leave it for now, and talk about it some other time?'

Mattis didn't answer, instead he nodded in the direction of the two aspen trees whose tops could only just be seen, one of them shattered by lightning.

The man wanted to get on.

'Well, if you can't even tell me what it is, then I'm afraid—'

'I'm nodding,' Mattis explained, interrupting him.

'Well?'

'Do you see what I'm nodding at?'

'The forest.'

'Not the *whole* forest,' said Mattis, looking straight at the aspen trees.

'Ah, then I think I know what it is,' said the haymaker, embarrassed all of a sudden. Obviously a clever fellow, Mattis realized.

'Then you're really sharp-witted,' he said to the haymaker. 'That made it easy for me.'

The man could have no idea what high praise he was receiving from Mattis. But the important thing for Mattis now was to choose his words carefully.

'Do you see the one and do you see the other?' he asked, quite pleased with himself.

'Yes.'

'But do you see what the lightning's done to one of them?'

'Oh my word yes!' said the clever fellow.

Now the way was open.

'But who *is* it?'

The question was put, but that was the end of it, too. A change came over the man.

'I don't know what you're talking about now,' he replied bluntly, unwilling to continue the conversation.

Mattis groaned. The man obviously knew only too well what he meant. That was why he was unwilling to go on.

'It's the one who's sitting at home now, isn't it?' Mattis asked, horrified at the sin he was committing. He was doing something wicked and dreadful, he knew it.

'Who's what?' said the haymaker, looking lost.

This was beginning to unnerve Mattis. Who's what? Yes, who's what! He dared not think about it.

'No, nothing!' he said frightened. 'I didn't mean it the way you think! She's sitting making coffee, there's nothing wrong. She's sitting making coffee like all the others!'

The haymaker got up from the guard-stone, clearly unwilling to listen.

'Well, I must be getting home. Tomorrow's another day, you know.'

But once again temptation got the better of Mattis—close as he was to a solution. He had to try asking in a roundabout way.

'*Is* there a name for one and a name for the other?'

'Don't know.'

The haymaker said it as bad-temperedly as he could, putting a stop to further questions. And off he went.

Mattis was left behind as uncertain as ever, and horrified at his own words. He didn't dare to ask anyone else about it.

26

Deep down inside Mattis was in no doubt that it was Hege, the aspen Hege, on which the lightning had left its mark. Hege was the elder of them, too. But he wouldn't admit that these were *his* thoughts—some wicked person was thinking for him at moments like this.

'Life is uncertain now,' he said to Hege, 'uncertain both for you and me.'

'What do you mean?' Hege asked. A lifetime together with Mattis had made her used to asking questions like this.

'I can't tell you, but it's awful,' he answered. 'When I said uncertain I mean something awful.'

'Oh, I expect we'll manage just as we've always done,' said Hege. 'I'm getting more orders than I can cope with.'

He realized that her thoughts had immediately gone to money and food.

'Are you talking about food?'

'I jolly well have to.'

Mattis was flabbergasted. He could see shadows closing in on Hege. He had to warn her.

'Do you remember the bird that got shot?'

'Yes.'

'But it isn't that either,' he said.

Hege remained silent, waiting.

'But it's only to do with one of us, the thing I mean!' he said earnestly.

'Well, I expect we'll manage somehow, whatever it is,' said Hege casually. 'But really, Mattis,' she said with a toss of the head, 'you think up so many strange things these days that I hardly recognize you.'

This testimony made him light up with joy. Hege knew how to make you happy when she wanted to. He went and sat down by himself to be alone with his joy.

Sitting there all on his own he gave a sudden start: I hadn't thought of *that*! If she's the bird, he said, putting it another way, what'll become of me?

I hadn't thought of that.

It looks bad whichever way I think about it.

He pushed the thought out of his mind as quickly as he could, and returned to Hege and said: 'Let's forget the whole thing.'

'I quite agree,' said Hege.

27

Mattis had plugged and repaired his boat and made it fit for use again. He was doing a lot of rowing this summer, caught a few miserable small fish—but most of the time he just rowed round and about on the big lake, down towards unfamiliar shores. The rowing always went well: his thoughts went straight down to the oars in orderly lines, they didn't get confused as they did when he was working on land.

There was something new out on the lake this summer. The spirits of Anna and Inger haunted the open water. There was no hope of meeting them—and yet who could tell? Why shouldn't they come out from one of the inlets, large as life, and see him. Come round a headland, beautiful and real. He asked for no more.

He rowed out on to the lake open and ready to receive them.

They didn't turn up.

Back at the cottage he walked up to Hege: 'Don't you find things different now, either?'

She didn't answer. But he could see that his words had disturbed her this time.

'Should I?'

He stood staring at her.

'Maybe,' he answered. 'No one can tell. Let me look into your eyes, Hege.'

No, she wouldn't let him. What was it she was afraid he might see? Suddenly he was afraid too. Was it anything to do with him?

'You mustn't leave me!' he shouted.

Now she looked up.

'Shan't leave you, Mattis. I'd have done it long ago in that case.'

Normally this would have been enough to reassure him, but today things were different. He had lost his peace of mind. And then there was this eternal knitting!

'Put it down for a bit!' he said, grabbing hold of the sweater and throwing it along the bench. Then he seized Hege by the wrist.

A frightened look came into her eyes.

'What on earth's got into you?'

'You mustn't go!' was all he said.

Waves of confused thoughts swept through him: it was the tree Hege the lightning had struck, he himself had decided this to save his own life. This could mean that Hege was in deadly peril. He'd seized hold of Hege and pulled her up on her feet. She didn't offer any resistance, as if she knew this outburst was bound to come some day.

'Come outside.'

She went outside with him.

'We can't stay here either. We must go far away. As far as possible!' he said, frightened and confused.

'In that case we can't leave at once, we must take food and things with us,' said Hege calmly.

'What?'

The calmness of her voice knocked him completely off balance.

'If we're going far we must get ready first, you know.'

She talked as if it were the most natural thing in the world for them to be leaving. In his agitated state of mind he didn't query it. Then suddenly he realized it was he who'd been talking nonsense.

'Come for a walk with me, then, if nothing else!' he pleaded. 'A little way into the forest, if nothing else!'

This she agreed to straight away.

'Come on then, Mattis.'

Mattis's conscience was torturing him.

'You don't know what I've done to you, Hege,' he said, 'but it's something dangerous. You must take good care, so you can stay alive.'

Hege couldn't help giving a start.

'Do stop it now, Mattis. I don't know what's the matter with you today. There's no reason why we shouldn't both of us go on living for a long time yet.'

'Something's been *done* about that,' Mattis said with great difficulty, 'I can't tell you about it.'

Hege had scarcely ever seen him like this before, so wretched. Now it was she who seized hold of his hand.

'Come on, let's go. I *am* coming for a walk with you today. Don't stand there like that.'

Without any definite idea of where they were going they strode off towards the cluster of spruces between the lake and the road; there was a little footpath there.

But Mattis had to go on from where he'd been interrupted, had to confess to the thing that was racking his conscience.

'And it's me who's done it,' he said, 'but I can't tell you about it. It's simply like I say.'

'Yes, yes, I know,' said Hege, trying to calm him down. 'I don't want to hear about it. So it's quite all right, do you understand? All right then, let's have no more of it.'

'Do you really mean it?' he said, full of gratitude.

They were walking fast, as if they were in a hurry to get to someone. Remorse drove Mattis on, and Hege had to follow. They passed the bog where Mattis and the woodcock had talked the language of the birds. Mattis didn't mention it at all; any expression of doubt from Hege would have spoilt it. They left the bog behind them and entered thicker forest. They were walking on real woodland floor now, no grass on the ground, just brown needles and patches of green moss.

'Let's stop a bit!' said Hege, sensing the silence of the forest. He did stop, at long last, and at once he felt the gentle silence too.

'Where are we?' he asked confused.

'Not far from home,' she said patiently. 'Just a little way inside the forest. Don't you recognize the place?'

He paid no attention.

'I feel awful,' he said instead. 'I'm so dreadfully sorry about something I've done.'

'Mattis, didn't you hear what I said: stop it!'

'Yes, but—'

'Not another word about it. You heard me say everything was all right, didn't you?'

'It doesn't feel like it,' said Mattis stubbornly.

'Sit down on that hump there!' Hege burst out in sheer desperation. There was a soft, round, moss-grown hump just where they happened to be standing.

Mattis sat down against his will. It was Hege who wanted him to, and she was the one with both will-power and strength.

'You've almost worn me out,' she said, standing beside him and drawing in great gulps of air.

Mattis had fallen quiet, and gave no answer. They went on sitting on the little hump. Not a sound was to be heard in the forest around them, and their own thumping hearts regained a calmer beat. Mattis sat next to Hege in the forest, silent, because he had started thinking about something quite new, something pleasanter than the things that had been upsetting him a moment ago.

'Now if you'd been a girl—' he blurted out, but stopped himself quickly. 'Rubbish!' he said. 'Of course you're a girl! I mean some other girl.'

'Do sit still now,' said Hege. 'Really, the way you're behaving today. You must stop it now.'

Since Mattis already seemed to have recovered, it was
quite natural for Hege to use this ordinary tone of voice,
chiding and scolding him a little. But Mattis put a stop
to it :

'You didn't dare to look at me you were so frightened,'
he said, banishing his vision of the girl.

'Afraid of you? I'm no more afraid of you than I am of
a cat. You know that. Now let's sit here for a bit, and stop
being sorry about the things we've done.'

She was stern. She gave him strength.

She added : 'You haven't got anything to be sorry
about, Mattis. There may be others who have, though.'

Mattis felt relieved. Hege was the clever one, you had
to admit it. There was no one quite like her for taking the
load off your mind.

He said full of gratitude : 'You don't know how nice
this is, Hege.'

'Nice here on this hump,' he added.

Hege looked as if she thought it was nice, too.

'We'll come here more often,' said Mattis.

But their time on the hump was up : Hege said sternly :
'We must go now.'

All the same Hege did something Mattis hadn't expected, she didn't rush straight back to her sweaters,
instead she said : 'We'll take a little time off, after all this.
It hasn't been easy for either of us.'

'No, it hasn't,' said Mattis. 'But you managed everything
all right. Shall we walk on a bit, then?'

His face lit up with joy at this unexpected suggestion
of hers.

The floor of the forest was like a carpet. They walked
on it quietly without saying a word. But it wasn't a very
wide forest, suddenly they found themselves at the edge of

141

the lake. The big lake where Anna and Inger had been.

The surface was like a mirror, and Mattis said : 'We were out there rowing for a whole day.'

Hege didn't ask when, there was only one boat-trip in the whole world.

More or less by chance Hege made an important decision for Mattis as they stood there. She suggested that he ought perhaps to go on rowing people about on the lake. It would be just the thing for him.

Mattis seized on the suggestion the moment it was thrown out, rather like catching a ball in the air : 'Yes, of course ! That's something I really can do !'

'Row girls across,' said Hege.

He sent her a quick glance.

'Do you think so?'

But Hege had to disillusion him : 'No, I'm afraid not. No one lives over there, it's just moorland, so there's no traffic across. But if there *had* been people living there, you could have been a ferryman.'

The idea struck him with full force. He wasn't listening to the things she was saying about no one living there.

'Yes, of course,' he said, talking to himself.

He would never have thought of anything like this himself. If Hege had said it to please him she'd picked on just the right thing. He fell silent, was lost in thought, didn't look where he was going and stumbled in the brushwood. Hege tried to chat a bit, but all she could get out of Mattis was hm—

'Let's go home now,' said Hege. 'The break's over as far as I am concerned.'

They walked along the shore in silence. Mattis led them to the place where he kept his boat.

'Are you going to stay down here?'

'Yes, you go on,' he answered, busy. 'I've got a lot to do to the boat now.'

Hege left him. When she was a little way up the slope, Mattis shouted to her, seemed to have got his breath back at last : 'Fancy not mentioning this before!'

Hege's only reply was a wave of the hand. Soon she was gone. But fancy not mentioning this before. Was she clever, or wasn't she? But what a wonderful end to all his worries today : he began to look forward to a job he could manage.

We won't give that lightning another thought, he said to himself. It isn't either of us that's meant! And maybe by tomorrow I'll have someone to row.

Now he was going to make the boat as decent as he possibly could, without spending any money on it.

Mattis worked until darkness fell. It was late July and the evenings were long. Mattis was no better at carpentry than anything else, but he worked lovingly on the boat that afternoon—with the poor tools he had at his disposal. When Hege asked, she learnt that he was to begin the very next day. Begin what? What you said, of course! Rowing people across the lake.

'It's the best idea you've ever had !' he finished.

Hege had to tell him the truth.

'I didn't mean it seriously, you know. There isn't anyone to row across.'

'You're not going to be like that, are you?' he said angrily, but by no means crushed. 'Are you trying to fool me?'

'I *said* there wasn't anyone.'

Then she reflected, and added quickly : 'Actually, now I come to think of it you ought to have a go. No harm in trying for a while. It'll keep you busy, too.'

Her words seemed like a distant murmur to Mattis, something that didn't concern him. She didn't realize what she'd started. For his own part he felt a turning point had

143

been reached. A way was opening up before him.

He only stopped working after the blows of the hammer had turned his thumb black and blue. It was so dark by then that he no longer saw the difference between his thumb and the nails.

As he walked up the slope he reflected that it had been a good summer, even though the woodcock was lying under the stone.

Part Three

28

Ferryman from today. The thought sent a warm glow through Mattis.

The surface of the lake was like a mirror and it lay there waiting for him.

Hege had obviously been pressing the ferryman idea which had come tumbling so suddenly from her lips. And Mattis half understood why: she was glad she wouldn't have to see him wandering about here all day with nothing to do. Glad to get rid of him for a bit in fact. But Mattis was so grateful to her for her idea that the motives behind it didn't really upset him very much.

She made some sandwiches and wrapped them up.

'Is it all for me?'

'Well, it's got to last all day, hasn't it? Or are you thinking of coming back straight away?'

'No, no, of course not,' he said. It sounded as though he were making her a promise.

Hege told him about all the things a ferryman has to do when he's on duty, too.

'And even if nobody comes straight away and shouts for the ferryman, the ferryman just has to wait and wait.'

Mattis looked at her, and all of a sudden she started blushing. She had been caught out in something she didn't want to acknowledge.

'I suppose I row across where it's narrowest?' he asked when he was ready to go.

'Yes, I think that's what they do.'

'But suppose it isn't narrow anywhere? What can I do then?'

'Well, then you'll just have to call in here and there,' said Hege, and this was a decision that pleased him. His parting words were as they should be : 'See you this evening.'

Hege nodded.

Things were going smoothly.

Mattis sat down in the boat, placed the oars in their correct position—and then it was only a question of waiting.

On this side of the lake there was no sign of anyone who wanted to go across. But he had to keep an eye on both sides, so after a while he rowed out from the shore. He had no timetable to keep to, and it was exciting to try out the boat after all the repair work he'd done. And it was such a relief to have found a permanent job at long last. No more waiting till someone took pity on him on the farms, no more of those dreadful days trying to work with the strong and the clever ones. And a job like *this*, he thought, reaching forward and giving long pulls at the oars. As soon as I've earned enough money to buy a new boat I'll stop using this old hulk. The better the boat, the more people'll want to use it. And then perhaps the people I want to row *most of all* will come.

He rowed in a dead straight line. His thoughts didn't stray. I must have been born to row on a lake, he said to himself. Fancy wasting so much of my life on all sorts of other things.

I might just as well row right across and wait there for a while.

But as he drew close to the blue slopes of the western shore, he saw there was nobody waiting there either. Well, that was quite natural, seeing it was his first day. People would have to get to know about the new ferryman before they started queuing up for his services.

He rowed along slowly, close to the shore, to see if there

was any track leading down out of the forest. No. He would have to wait without a track—somewhere or other where the boat could be manoeuvred right on to the shore. The ferryman must always wait, those were Hege's words.

Mattis was feeling fine, lying contentedly in the bottom of the boat, and letting the sun shine straight into his face. The boat smelt strongly of tar, a pleasant smell that came from the new rags that had been pushed and nailed into place the evening before. The sun-baked shore had a faint, pleasant smell of its own.

Mattis stretched, happy and content.

And I'm fully employed as well! Lying here and loafing about.

He couldn't help laughing.

Lie there as long as he would, no one came. He pushed the boat out again and set course for his own shore. There might well be someone sitting there waiting by now. The news was bound to spread as time went on and people noticed he was rowing straight across, on a sort of regular service.

That's what it's like being a ferryman, you've got to be everywhere at once—but how can you?

He liked murmuring the word ferryman—that was what he was now, and it didn't sound at all bad. I bet there isn't a ferryman who rows straighter. You can't row straighter than straight. Pity the wake disappears so quickly, it ought to stay on the water for days, covering it with streaks.

There wasn't anyone on his own shore either, when he finally got there. He would have liked to have taken five minutes off now, and nipped up to see Hege, but he resisted the temptation. He sat loyally on the shore eating his sandwiches. Hege shouldn't have any cause to be angry with him this time, he wouldn't be a burden to her any longer; here he was, eating his sandwiches.

Hush.

He listened.

In fact he'd been listening all the time. And wasn't someone calling, over from the hills in the west? He stopped chewing so he could hear better. Listened for a long time with his mouth full of bread. No, no one could shout across a lake as wide as that. And yet someone *was* shouting!

Mattis began rowing at once. Surely there was something familiar about the shout, too. It could have been Hege, but that was impossible for the simple reason that Hege was this side of the lake.

Hege's calling, far away on the other side, he mumbled, and suddenly he stopped dead.

Is someone calling?

A call like that on my very first day. Anyone who can shout across a lake this size, why, I'm almost frightened of them. But it *is* Hege—

Nonsense.

A good thing it isn't night. But I suppose they have to go out in the middle of the night, too, ferrymen. People call across the water in darkness as well as in light.

At least the calls had stopped now. Mattis heaved at the oars, arrived covered in sweat after so much hard work in the hot sun. That didn't matter. He was managing to cope with the ferrying, that was the main thing. His thoughts held the oars in their proper place.

But there was no one there. No one to be seen or heard. The hills on this side were long, gentle, tree-covered slopes, which reached a great height. It was all forest land, not a house anywhere. No one lived beyond the highest ridge, either, there was nothing but deserted moorland up there.

Who had been calling?

No one, of course, you can't shout right across the lake, he said in a stern voice. But there was something wrong here. Mattis took his job as ferryman so seriously that someone was bound to come down from the hillside soon. Ferrymen had to meet people like this. The hillside lay deserted. Who was it shouted so loud that the sound carried farther than an ordinary voice?

Perhaps the ferryman had to give a signal himself? He got up from his seat and shouted hey! in a loud and frightened voice. It wasn't an easy thing to do.

The echo answered, no one else.

'Here I am!' Mattis shouted at the mysterious hillside which held a thousand secrets.

No, no one came down. No one needed a ferry on this side of the lake.

This wasn't as it should be.

Yes, but Hege did say it was a question of waiting and waiting, he tried to comfort himself.

But somebody was calling me!

He listened so intently that everything else, too, seemed somehow to die away to an attentive whisper.

Then came a call from the other side of the lake. From his own shore. The voice to whom distance meant nothing. And once again it was Hege's lonely voice, calling for the ferry, or whatever it was.

'All right!' he answered in trembling tones, swinging his wretched little boat round. But it's a long way!

Must be because it's my first day, he thought in bewilderment.

Once again he was on his way. But progress was slow, after all, he couldn't row at top speed the whole time. But everyone'll get across all the same, he promised.

He was still keeping a dead straight line. Nothing wrong

with his rowing. He pulled and tugged at the oars, arrived back at his own shore, saw with horror that there was no one waiting there. Nothing but the familiar, deserted stretch of beach at the bottom of the slope below the cottage. He gulped. This filled him with fear. The familiar shore filled him with fear and panic. There was only one thing to do now: get back home to Hege. He refused to believe that it was really she who'd been calling him.

Mattis secured the boat and hurried up the hill. Didn't feel like looking behind him.

Hege was busy knitting, as calm as could be. She didn't show any sign of irritation at seeing her brother back so soon. She just said: 'Home already?'

'It's not like you think!' he said. 'There's something odd going on on the lake today.'

'Odd?'

'You've been calling down there!' he said, hysterically. 'What do you say to that?'

'Don't talk nonsense, Mattis.'

'As soon as I'm on one side, there's a call from the other! And it's your voice. Right across the lake. Is that odd or isn't it?'

'There are no calls like that,' she said quickly. She was disturbed, that was obvious.

'But you know how good I am at hearing things,' said Mattis.

'No, you're just too keen on this ferrying job of yours and you imagine you're hearing all kinds of things. You don't want to listen for things that aren't there, you know. Just you go back and carry on as before. There's nothing odd out on the lake.'

Her words had a soothing effect on him.

'I wasn't thinking of giving up.'

'I know. Off with you now.'

Thus comforted, he went back down to the lake. But no sooner had he reached the boat than he began listening. And very soon he heard all sorts of strange sounds. Above them all came the sound he *wanted* to hear: the call for the ferry, commanding, inquiring and in Hege's voice, just as before.

It must be because I've got a permanent job for the first time in my life, he thought. That's why I can't help hearing all sorts of things. That's what Hege said, too.

And a call for the ferry was what he wanted to hear, after all. He couldn't really understand why those who were calling didn't show themselves, but that was bound to alter soon.

It was a real strain. They want to put me to the test my first day, he thought. And I shan't fail!

He swung the boat round and set course for the distant hills in the west, another tiring trip across.

There were no calls to be heard.

At long last he arrived at the other side, his arms aching. Was prepared to find the shore deserted and every kind of terror waiting for him. The day had begun with fun and laughter—now it was tense and tiring. But a test was a test—the boat grated against the bottom, and Mattis stood erect and mastered the unfamiliar situation.

He turned towards the mysteries of the deserted shore in an effort to make them reveal themselves.

'Give a call, if you're there!' he shouted up at the hillside. He was tired out and crazy with suspense, forced himself up on to his toes so he stood taller and straighter than usual, leant on the oars, ready to push off at once if whatever appeared should prove too horrible.

'Come out!' he said.

No one came. The hillside lay before him with a thousand hiding places. He was becoming frantic, grew white-faced and frightened because no one came.

153

'Here I am!' he yelled. His feeble head couldn't take any more.

'Right-oh!' came the reply at last. High up on the tree-covered hillside. A single word of reply.

Mattis jumped as if he had been stung. This wasn't Hege, this was no mystery voice—it was a real person like himself, the call of a man.

Who have I called?

Well, it's a real person at least.

It was quiet up there now, but there was a man on his way down.

Mattis stood in the same position as before, ready to flee at short notice. No one told him that this wasn't the way for a ferryman to behave. He pushed the boat out and lay bobbing up and down close to the shore with his oars out of the water.

I bet ferrymen often have to sit like this, he said to himself as an excuse.

Oh no! he thought from time to time. Oh no!

Meanwhile the unknown person was coming down the hillside, hidden by the forest. After all the shouting this felt uncanny, too, although it was natural enough. But it was no doubt a test, and Mattis was determined not to fail.

'Here!' he shouted, to give his position.

'All right,' came the reply, much nearer than before.

A man's voice.

There he was.

Suddenly a man emerged from the shrubs at the edge of the forest and stood in full view on the shore. He caught sight of Mattis, waved to him and came across.

Mattis sat for a bit letting his ridiculous fears trickle gently away, like the rain running off a hat. What had he expected to see?

The person coming towards him was as ordinary as could be: a man with a rucksack. Mattis let the boat bump against the shore, stern foremost, to make it easy for the man to get in. It was wonderful to be a ferryman for the first time.

'It's the ferryman you're looking for, I suppose?' he said eagerly, before the stranger had uttered a word. 'That's my job on this lake.'

The stranger looked pleased.

'Yes, things have turned out very well,' he said. 'The weather was so nice today that I came straight over the mountains, and what I thought I'd do was walk along by the lake till I reached habitation. Then I reckoned I could get someone to row me across if I paid them. I didn't realize it was *so* desolate on this side, I've never been here before.'

'There's a proper ferry service here from today,' said Mattis. 'It's my very first day. And you're my very first passenger. Do you want to go straight across? My home's straight across from here. Well, and Hege lives there too, of course.'

Mattis was so happy he forgot to explain what he was talking about. The man didn't seem to care much, either.

'It's all the same to me,' he answered a bit crossly. 'But take the shortest route. That is, if this boat'll take two? I'm not sure whether it will. So I wouldn't really call it a proper ferry boat.'

While he was talking disparagingly about the boat, he got in and took off his heavy rucksack. An axe handle stuck up by the flap—the man was probably a lumberjack coming to look for work. A really fine lumberjack—with muscles that tore his shirt sleeve perhaps? That was what he looked like.

'Give me a chance,' said Mattis. 'You can't expect me to have made enough money to buy a new boat if you're my first passenger. I haven't earned a penny so far.'

'What d'you live on, then?' said the man. The answer clearly didn't interest him, he'd half turned away from Mattis and was just letting himself be ferried. Mattis was able to take a good look at him. The way he spoke showed that he came from a long way off. As for age he might be about as old as Mattis himself or perhaps a bit older. His face was neither handsome nor anything else, it just was. He was no tramp as far as clothes were concerned. Everything was just as it should be. The first thing that was obvious was that he was one of the strong and clever ones —like everyone else. But anyway, Mattis was rowing and he was happy.

'How old are you?' he asked.

'Forty-three, why?'

'Nothing,' said Mattis, he would have liked to have said how old he was, but the tone of the other man's voice stopped him.

'I might have known it!' said the stranger, angry all of a sudden, grabbing his rucksack which now lay in a pool of water. The boat had been plugged recently, it was true, but only well enough for one person apparently. With two in it fresh cracks sank below the water line, at the same time as the pressure increased.

Mattis didn't dare to offer any excuses. The boat was letting in water, and the clever stranger had reacted sharply enough. Mattis hurriedly changed the subject, and asked: 'Had you lost your way then, seeing you came down in a place where there was no road?'

The stranger had explained all this before, but now he answered with a sneer: 'I couldn't have lost my way, could I, ending up just by the ferry like that?'

My word, this chap was sharp-witted all right. There he was again: 'Have you got a scoop though, or anything of that sort? We're not meant to swim, are we?'

Mattis bent his head. The boat wasn't good enough. He brought out the scoop, and the man started bailing. He looked pretty angry. Mattis felt exhausted and was rowing slowly, but he kept a straight line.

They got across. Just before they reached land, the man started speaking again; it was a long time since he'd said anything.

'Can you help me find somewhere to stay for the night? I'm tired, mind, I don't want to have to go far.'

His last words sounded almost like a complaint against Mattis, because he'd taken so long to cross the lake.

'You can stay with us, seeing the boat let in so much water,' Mattis mumbled shamefacedly.

'Where do you live, then?'

'Here, of course,' said Mattis, pointing up at the little cottage in the hollow.

'Well,' said the man, in a slightly more friendly tone, 'that would be the best solution, if I could.'

'The best solution?' Mattis repeated. His attitude towards the man changed all of a sudden.

'I've come here to try and get work as a lumberjack,' said the stranger. He was in a more friendly mood now, too.

They arrived. The clever stranger no doubt saw what a ramshackle house it was. At the same time his eyes took a quick look at Mattis. Hege was sitting outside with her work. She stared at them in friendly surprise.

'I've rowed him across,' said Mattis, 'on my very first day! But gosh am I tired!'

'Good evening,' said the stranger, 'do you think it would be possible to stay the night here?'

'I've promised him he can already,' said Mattis who wanted to be in on this too. 'He can sleep in the empty room in the attic, can't he?'

Hege was a little bewildered. This was something new.

She seemed to be pleased about it, the look she gave the traveller was friendly and curious.

'I've promised him something to eat, too,' said Mattis, although he hadn't done anything of the sort.

'Do you know one another, then?' Hege asked her brother.

'No,' said the man.

'No, he didn't say anything while we were rowing across,' said Mattis, 'didn't even tell me his name. He was too busy bailing.'

The man stepped forward and gave his name as Jørgen.

'But I've got food here in my rucksack,' he said, 'you don't need to bother about that.'

'I promised him something to eat!' said Mattis obstinately.

A room, food, stay here perhaps? Hege was both bewildered and excited. Mattis began to feel proud of the fact that he was the cause of all this, he followed Hege into the house and told her more about Jørgen: 'He's clever, too,' he said to her. 'You're not angry with me for this, are you Hege?'

Mattis was simply fishing, he could see very well that Hege wasn't angry at all. Something had come over her, she was tense, she crossed the floor in a different way.

'Maybe there'll be someone else to row across tomorrow,' said Mattis. 'If only I could bring someone home to you every day! But it was quite a strain, I can tell you.'

Hege climbed up the ladder to get the attic room ready. Mattis sat down next to Jørgen in the room below. Neither of them said anything. Mattis was so tired that he couldn't sit straight.

29

As it turned out, Jørgen didn't leave at once. He got work
straight away in the forest close by—so he asked if it'd be
all right if he just stayed on in the attic. Mattis and Hege
said yes, surprised and happy. Hege most of all.

Hege was different already; Mattis couldn't help noticing it, and he noticed that he was different, too.

Jørgen had his own, curt way of behaving. When he got
back from the forest he pottered about in the kitchen for
a little while, cooking his dinner. Then he climbed up the
ladder to his own room, to rest. He didn't try and make
friends with the other two. But brother and sister never
ceased to be amazed. Someone had come to their house
and wanted to stay.

In addition Mattis had his job as ferryman. He was at it
every day. But he never repeated his first success—in fact
there was never anyone who wanted to be taken across.
Sometimes motor-boats went chugging over towards the
western hills and came back again and went somewhere
else, but this was something that went on outside Mattis's
world. Mattis was a proper ferryman with a rowing-boat,
and he had his job even if there was no one to ferry—and
he'd stopped hearing imaginary calls and shouts now. He
soon got into the habit of dozing off while he waited by
one of the shores. He made a couple of journeys across
every day, provided there wasn't too much wind; and anyway the boat was just about right for *one*, it didn't let in
too much water like that. It was wonderful to have a job

he could manage, and that Hege approved of. It wasn't his fault that nobody came to use the ferry.

The only thing that was wrong, of course, was that he wasn't earning any money for his new boat, but things could easily improve. Each new day could bring a whole load of passengers.

On top of all this, Jørgen had settled down with them, and looked as if he intended to stay.

One day Mattis said: 'Now we're like other people.'

Hege wasn't pleased.

'Don't be so stupid! Of course we're like other people, and so we always have been.'

'Yes,' he said meekly.

'I don't want to hear that sort of talk, Mattis.'

Hege was different in many ways, Mattis felt. She wasn't as kind to him as she used to be. Now and then she looked at him with an expression he couldn't fathom.

'Oh, I wish you wouldn't behave like that,' she said every so often, when he'd done something that wasn't as clever as it might have been.

'What's the matter with you these days?' he asked unhappily. 'What are you so cross for? I'm the same as I've always been, but you're cross.'

She shrugged her shoulders.

'Don't talk nonsense.'

'I'd have expected something quite different,' said Mattis, gazing steadily at her. 'I wouldn't have expected you to be at all cross, but still.'

'What exactly do you mean, Mattis? I don't understand you.'

'You don't want me to say it *now*, do you?' he asked, hesitant and reluctant.

'All right, then stop this nonsense.' They both withdrew.

Mattis certainly noticed how much attention Hege paid

to Jørgen, the strong and clever lumberjack. Jørgen on the other hand just walked past, smelling of the forest and saying nothing, or at the most commenting on the weather. In the evening he returned, bringing the smell of the forest back with him. Hege asked if she could help him with one or two things in the kitchen? No, he was used to managing on his own. And Hege had to leave again. He didn't talk about himself, either. If the subject was mentioned he pretended not to hear. Or he said : Does it really matter? But don't worry, I haven't done anything wrong.

Hege sent him furtive glances. Mattis noticed the way Hege's face sometimes changed beyond recognition, came alive and was full of expression—and the slightest thing made her irritable. I'd have expected something quite different, he told her.

30

Mattis carried on rowing in the same way, day after day. No one came to use the ferry, but ferrymen have to remain at their post just the same, waiting.

He didn't dislike it. On the other hand he liked his sister less and less. She grew worse with every day that passed. She was always keeping a watch on him. Almost everything he said or did was wrong. As soon as they were alone she started nagging him.

'Really,' she kept on saying, 'that's not the way to do things. Do please try and remember.'

She dressed more neatly than before. He noticed that she often stood prinking herself instead of spending every available minute on the eight-petalled roses.

He noticed that her whole appearance was smarter—

and he rather liked it. Girls *were* smart looking. Yet it made him feel uneasy.

'Going somewhere?'

She gave a start, she'd been so absorbed.

'No.'

'What are you making yourself up for, then?'

'No particular reason.'

'But I can't take a step without you snooping around after me,' she added.

He felt ashamed; what she said was true.

But she wanted to be more beautiful than she was before, so much was obvious. She was making herself more beautiful for the lumberjack. Why? I won't think about it! he decided.

It didn't look as if it made much impression on Jørgen, Mattis was glad to see. Jørgen worked in the forest, and looked after himself at home, and never came out of his shell.

There's no danger.

Won't think about it.

Mattis pushed it aside with both hands.

One Saturday evening Jørgen came rushing down the ladder and made straight for Mattis. Mattis had spent the day rowing about in an empty boat as usual. Now it was after supper. Mattis was in the main room, Hege in her bedroom. I bet she's standing in front of the mirror, Mattis thought bitterly. Outside the moon was shining. Then Jørgen came clattering down from his room with unusual speed. Mattis held his breath.

Jørgen came towards him: 'I think you'll have to go out on the lake!'

Mattis jumped up: 'Was there a call?'

Just then Hege came in. Smart.

Jørgen looked somehow surprised, perplexed by something he'd heard.

'I'm not quite sure—yes I think there must have been —someone calling who wants to be rowed across.'

Mattis felt the excitement pulsating through him.

'So it's come at last,' he said softly.

Jørgen stood looking at him, full of urgency.

So now it had come, the night journey Mattis had been dreading and had pictured in his mind time and time again. The sort of thing a ferryman had to be prepared for.

'I'm sure that's right, what you heard, Jørgen,' he said, 'I knew I'd have to make a trip at night sooner or later. Hege said the same.'

As usual he looked across at Hege. She had her back to him, went quickly over to the window and looked out at the moonlight.

'Yes, I'm afraid you ferrymen always have to be on call,' said Jørgen. 'When someone shouts, you just have to go.'

Mattis nodded. He got ready with a certain amount of ceremony, put on a warm sweater, and one or two other things. Then he stood in front of Jørgen and in front of Hege's back : 'You must expect me when I arrive, that's about all I can say. But it'll be quite some time, I'm sure.'

'Yes, you'll have to make a trip across,' said Jørgen, 'even if there's no one down on this side.'

Mattis strode out.

He was frightened. But he was determined not to run away in front of Jørgen. He was going out on the lake, he'd show him.

Outside a bloodshot autumn moon shone down on the green grass. Beautiful beyond description. Mattis noticed it, but he couldn't stop now, he got straight into the boat. There was no one standing there, and there was no one to be heard—he was going entirely on what Jørgen had said when he set out. But someone as clever as Jørgen was bound to be right.

A gentle wind was blowing. Small waves gurgled among the pebbles and glittered in the moonlight.

But supposing the boat doesn't make it? It was touch and go when Jørgen came. Since then nobody but me's been in it.

He'll just have to bail, my passenger, *whoever he is.* And he's no ordinary person, he thought.

You don't know what they may be like, the sort of people who hail the ferry at night. But whoever he is, I'll row him *straight,* I'll show him. I'll show them all! said Mattis defiantly, and started off.

Out on the lake the red moon looked smaller. But it was so lovely here that you almost wanted to be a night-ferryman for the rest of your life, and sleep during the day.

Mattis rested on his oars, letting the glistening blades hover above the water. He listened in the direction of the shore. Then he started rowing again. He rowed slowly, was waiting to hear where the calls were coming from.

There were no calls. But it was bound to be over by the western hills, he told himself. He began rowing in that direction. And time went by. Before he realized it the hill-side was almost on top of him. He'd rowed right across without hearing a sound.

With the hillside up above a sinking feeling came over him, rather as it did before a storm. But he rowed right up to the shore, and the boat rubbed against the sandy bottom.

I must let him know I'm here now.

No, I don't dare. Surely I've done enough, rowing across in the pitch dark.

But the voice of all ferrymen said : I'm afraid you must,

Mattis. Tell him you've come. Now you're the ferryman here.

'Ho-y!' It was uttered in a trembling voice, and with a peculiar little catch in the middle. He was beginning to break out in a cold sweat, too. He sat hunched up in the boat instead of standing up strong and straight and shouting.

There aren't many who'd change places with me now, he thought.

The hillside was silent.

Give another shout, Mattis, or—

'Hoy!' he said miserably.

In among the trees a bird shrieked.

That was enough in the mood Mattis was in now. He plunged his oars into the water and rowed away from the shore leaving a trail of foam behind him. He was shaking with fear, rowing blindly. It was only when he was far out that he stopped, and waited for the panic to subside. He sat for a bit gasping for breath.

Well, there was certainly no one there who wanted the ferry. We've been fooled, both Jørgen and me, he thought. But who is it that's doing it?

On the journey back across he rowed slowly and gently, bewildered and deep in thought. Around him the night was as beautiful as ever.

At this late hour Hege came out on the steps to meet him, all alone. Hadn't she gone to bed? What was going on? Here she was, fully dressed.

'Anything the matter, Hege?'

She shook her head.

'I'm glad you've come back at last,' she said.

She must have been sitting up worrying about him. A feeling of warmth swept through him.

He followed her into the main room where there was a

light on. And there he stopped in complete surprise : he hadn't noticed it out in the moonlight, but now he could see the expression of naked happiness on Hege's face.

'Mattis,' she said, for no particular reason.

'What is it?'

'Don't know,' she said.

He felt a sense of peace and gratitude, he'd got a good sister who sat up waiting for him till he was safely back from his adventure on the lake.

'You could have gone to bed, you know,' he said, 'it wasn't as dangerous as it looked.'

'What?' Hege stammered.

'What's the matter now, then?' he asked, too. She was so strange all of a sudden, avoiding his gaze.

'I'm glad you sat up waiting for me all the same,' he said gratefully.

She nodded to him, but the strange expression remained.

'You must never leave me !' he said suddenly.

She gave no reply. He didn't feel it was necessary, either.

31

In the morning Mattis noticed the way Hege followed Jørgen with her eyes, more closely than before. When Jørgen was in the room, she saw nothing else. Mattis didn't like this, and went up to the lumberjack as he was about to leave.

'You must have made a mistake last night, I went out on a fool's errand.'

'Oh,' said Jørgen.

And he set off for the forest.

That was the end of it. Jørgen was unapproachable somehow. Hege sat in the background. She had stopped knitting and was keeping a watchful eye on the two men. But the moment Jørgen left, her fingers returned to their usual busy movements.

Everything was just as it always had been, and yet it wasn't as it always had been. Mattis sat thinking about it and reached this conclusion.

I need some sweets, he thought after a bit.

He wanted to go straight away, he really needed them after all he'd been through, but when he mentioned the subject of money and the store, Hege said no.

'I do the shopping myself now. I've been doing it for some time, you know that.'

Yes, it was true, she had. He'd been busy ferrying every day.

'You've got your job as ferryman now,' Hege went on, 'and that's more than enough for you. And people only ask you all sorts of questions when you go to the store.'

'No they don't!'

'Don't they? Well they might—and it's no business of theirs, d'you hear?'

There was such a tone of finality in her voice, that he didn't utter a word of protest. And she'd been so strangely happy when he arrived back home safe and sound last night. Come to that, there was a look of happiness on her face today, too.

A little later she produced a packet of sandwiches.

'Jørgen's forgotten his lunch,' she said anxiously. 'I'd better take it to him.'

'I'll do that,' said Mattis. 'I know exactly where he is.'

'No, you must get on with your ferrying,' said Hege. 'You can't just leave it like that.'

Then Mattis came out with what was on his mind : 'It's

awful, the way you can never take your eyes off Jørgen. Not for a single day.'

Hege stood still for a moment.

'What do you mean?' she said, to gain time.

'I don't like it,' Mattis went on. 'You must take your eyes off Jørgen.'

Hege laughed.

'Haven't you got your eyes fixed on anything, then, Mattis?' she said, winking. 'What about Anna and Inger?'

'Oh, that's different,' he was about to say, but said it in another way instead: 'Well, *in that case* you can look at Jørgen to your heart's content.' His happiness was returning. How clever and good she is, he thought; she'd really noticed about him and Anna and Inger.

Hege set off for the forest with the sandwiches, and Mattis for his part went to do some ferrying.

Down on the shore Mattis had many new thoughts—they were about eyes under stones: There's lid upon lid and stone upon stone, but it can never be hidden.

The surface of the lake was broad. He looked out across it. Dimly he thought: help Mattis.

Why!

He gave a start.

No, no, he mumbled meaninglessly, and seized the oars. Lead in the wing, he thought, and there's stone upon stone, over the eyes.

32

Jørgen didn't leave—and this had its compensations. He earned good money working in the forest, and he paid

Hege well. Mattis was happy and unhappy at the same time; deep down inside him there was a gnawing fear. Both the good things and the bad were his doing : for it was he who'd brought the lumberjack to the house in the first place. He wondered if Jørgen would come and sit with them on Sunday, but Jørgen stayed up in his room in the attic, or sat down on the shore somewhere all alone. Hege didn't go after him, Mattis watched her carefully to see if she would.

The next Sunday arrived. Jørgen was in his room as usual.

Mattis was bursting to talk.

'Hege,' he began in a fumbling voice. He had to find out more about her and Jørgen.

And she really let him have it : 'I'm fed up with you staring at me!' she burst out. For once there was genuine fury in her voice. 'I can't take a step without you staring!' she said.

Her words went through him like a knife. Fed up with him? She'd actually said she was fed up with him.

She regretted it almost as soon as it was said—as usual when she'd lost her temper. She became more gentle again : 'Please try and forget it, Mattis. It's not true, I'm not fed up with you.'

'How can I forget it if you've said it?' Mattis replied horrified.

Hege stood in front of him, frightened : 'Sometimes you have to ask people to forget things you've said all the same. Haven't you ever felt like that? I didn't want to—'

'I know what it is,' said Mattis suddenly.

'What is it you know? How can you know anything when there's nothing to know?' Hege answered quickly. 'I'm not fed up with you.'

Heavens! she's sharp all right, he thought, but he'd been sharper this time, he'd been talking about Jørgen and well she knew it, she couldn't fool him. He'd been turning it all over in his mind while he'd been out ferrying these last few days. If she was fed up with him, it was because of Jørgen. And now he had to find out about it, there was nothing else for it!

'Come down, Jørgen!' he called up to the attic suddenly, in a voice that was dangerously loud.

Hege shouted: 'Mattis! What on earth d'you think you're playing at?'

'Come down, Jørgen!'

Hege thought her brother had taken leave of his senses, she grabbed him by the arm to try and get him out of the room. At the same time she uttered threatening words in a low, angry voice: 'Shut up! Have you gone mad! What must he think of you? Come on, we're going outside. Can't you leave Jørgen in peace!'

'Jørgen!'

'It's nothing,' Hege shouted up to the attic.

'I can hear him coming now,' said Mattis, refusing to let himself be dragged outside.

Yes, Jørgen was on the ladder now.

Hege let go of Mattis, rushed into her room and shut the door behind her.

Jørgen came in and asked: 'What is it, Mattis? Here I am.'

Jørgen was in his Sunday best, a fine looking fellow and a terrific lumberjack. Mattis didn't answer his question, he stood rather taken aback by his own impetuous behaviour.

'What sort of a game is this?' said Jørgen rather sharply, coming nearer.

There was nothing for it but to have another go: 'I'm afraid you can't stay here any longer,' said Mattis, the colour rising in his cheeks. The words were out before he realized what was happening—they'd run through his mind countless times already.

'Really? What have I done then?' said Jørgen. He didn't sound very angry either, it was almost as though he accepted it.

'You mustn't take my sister away!' Mattis blurted out. Jørgen stood unmoved.

'I'm not going to take your sister anywhere. Nor am I going to leave the house, just when I've settled in.'

Mattis was momentarily at a loss.

'Hege isn't like she used to be, and it's your fault.'

'What do you mean? What's Hege been telling you?'

'Hege isn't—' Mattis began, but he stopped. He was going to say: isn't kind any longer, but he changed it to: isn't like she used to be, that's all!

The lumberjack forgot himself, and gave a little laugh.

His laughter had an instantaneous effect on Mattis. He became absolutely furious, all kinds of thoughts chased through his brain, before he realized what was happening he was giving the smug fellow a piece of his mind: 'There's no need for you to laugh! What do you know about the things I know? What do you know about the bird that was up on the path here—more wonderful than you'll ever know! But it was there. And it was for Hege's sake. I know a lot about Hege, a lot. And then you come along!'

Mattis almost collapsed at the force of his own words, and they were probably intended to crush Jørgen so completely that he'd never dare show his face here again.

But it didn't work that way.

'Yes, then I come along,' Jørgen answered calmly. 'By the way, where's Hege got to?'

Mattis pointed to her door.

'What are you doing?' he rapped out, seeing Jørgen making straight for her room.

171

'Wait a second, Mattis, we might just as well talk about this thing properly.'

And with that Jørgen went into Hege's room, and Mattis's outburst had been all for nothing. Inside the room a few hasty words were exchanged—then the door opened and Jørgen and Hege both came out. Jørgen obviously acting as Hege's protector. Hege looked shyly at her brother this time.

Jørgen put his arm round her short, plump body. Then he took her across to where Mattis was standing. Mattis could only gape. Hege was blushing.

'We're good friends, Hege and me,' said Jørgen, 'it's just as well you should know.'

Hege didn't resist, she was quite content to stand there with Jørgen's arm around her—happy on the one hand and frightened on the other.

Mattis asked with great difficulty: 'Are you really sweethearts?'

Hege looked up at last. She had given Mattis so many meals over the years that she felt she could.

'Yes, we are,' she said to him. And whether or not she'd intended it, her face lit up in a broad smile, broader than Mattis could ever remember.

Then she smiled in a different way, and said to him: 'And you were the person who ferried him across to me, remember.'

Mattis hardly heard what she was saying. He was gripped by a sudden fear. Hege was lost to him.

'When did you become sweethearts, then?' he asked weakly, yet insistently.

'While you were ferrying we became sweethearts.'

Mattis saw how happy Hege was, standing there with Jørgen's arm round her. Her face was hardly recogniz-able, no trace of tiredness or anger, no worry marked it. He felt quite overcome by it all, at first almost inclined to

be pleased, but then the full realization struck him : Hege
was lost.

No, no.

Surely you can see that. She's lost.

'Why didn't you tell me this before, then, Hege?' he
burst out at last.

'We wanted to be sure first,' said Hege. 'But you've
found out for yourself now as well. You've been clever.'

He started at this word of flattery she'd used to pacify
him. It made him writhe. He asked the question on which
everything seemed to hang.

'Are you going to go away?'

'Why should you think that?'

'Well, seeing you didn't dare tell me about it !'

'No,' Hege said firmly, 'we're not going away. There's
room for Jørgen here too. Everything'll be just as it was
before.'

Mattis hardly dared believe it, they'd hidden so much
from him. Fervently he said : 'I wish I'd never been in-
stalled as ferryman.'

'Now, now,' said Hege. 'You've got a good job, rowing
on that lake all day.'

'But Jørgen's the only one I've brought across ! I wish
I'd never taken it up.'

Jørgen had remained silent all the while. Now at last he
spoke.

'There may be others,' he said.

Mattis just shook his head. Jørgen went on : 'You never
know what may turn up—on the lake, you know.'

Mattis felt he had the right to be hard and merciless
now : 'I wish I'd never—'

He didn't get any further, Hege intervened before he
had a chance to damn and destroy anything. She walked
straight up to her brother and did something she'd never
done before as long as he could remember : she embraced

173

him, held him tightly in her arms. There was an odd expression on her face. And then she said : 'Bless you, Mattis, for becoming the ferryman.'

She released him again, quickly and rather shamefacedly, walked away, over to Jørgen.

Mattis had to ask himself : then why has she been getting so cross with me since she became Jørgen's sweetheart? Should he ask her? No.

'Well then, there must be different kinds of sweethearts,' he said instead, a little off the point.

They looked at him, were on their guard. Had he been too clever for them this time? he wondered. Hege asked : 'What do you mean, different kinds?'

'Just that this isn't the first time I've seen sweethearts, you know,' said Mattis. 'Last spring I was thinning out turnips with a couple, and they spent the whole time pinching each other's legs.'

Hege and Jørgen felt happy again, off their guard.

'They were younger,' said Hege, 'that's when they pinch each other.'

Jørgen remained silent.

'They were kind, too,' said Mattis, 'the whole time.'

'Yes, I'm sure they were,' said Hege.

'But why have you been so cross?'

There it came after all, tumbling out, because of what Hege had said. He couldn't take it back. Actually he was quite glad he'd said it.

Hege blinked, a little startled. Then she tried to cover up, without much success.

'Cross? I haven't been cross.'

This was no answer—Mattis had stumped her, he could see that. While he was in this strong position he said : 'I'm going down to my boat. I must think a lot more about this!'

'Yes,' said Hege.

He went at once.

Half-way down the slope he paused, stood thinking, went up a little way, then he turned abruptly and went back down again.

You my woodcockest bird—the phrase suddenly struck him.

He didn't push the boat out, sat down on the shore next to it, inhaling the pleasant tarry smell. But he looked at it with distaste, and thought : Who was most to blame for Jørgen's arrival, the boat or himself? Neither of them could have brought Jørgen across to the house alone.

33

Hege now began visiting Jørgen quite openly in the evening when he was resting. This was the first change that took place after the important announcement. And Mattis could see that Hege was full of happiness. He realized that he ought to be full of happiness as well, but he couldn't manage it, he was frightened.

He plucked up courage and asked : 'What are you going to do? Are you going to stay here?'

'We shan't decide anything about that for a long time yet,' Hege answered. 'We're going to leave things as they are for the moment.'

'But when will you know !'

'We'll see. Just stop worrying.'

Didn't she realize how frightened he was? What was going to become of him the day she left and wasn't around any longer? Hege'd been within arm's length all his life, he'd never known anything different.

'And then there was the bird up on the path,' he began but got no further.

'The one that got shot? What about it?'

'No, that one only got filled with lead.'

'Listen, Mattis, you oughtn't to think about these birds so much, leave the birds to look after themselves,' she said light-heartedly, as if ready to burst into song. She didn't, though; the expression in Mattis's eyes stopped her at once.

Mattis said gravely: 'I don't understand you.'

All song was gone, she said firmly: 'Try and act like a grown-up, Mattis. Use your common sense, the way grown-ups have to.'

'What *is* it, then?' he asked bitterly.

'Think of others a bit, too,' she said. 'You have to when you're grown-up.'

'What others?' he asked helplessly, filling her with fright.

She made no reply.

He set off to do a bit of ferrying. There's got to be a call from the lake soon, surely, he thought. Something or other's got to happen now.

Be grown-up, she said. She never used words like that in the old days.

He was plugging the holes in his boat. Every morning he had to inspect the tarred rags and the patchy repairs. His new boat was now more than ever a dream, vanishing into the distance.

Be grown-up?

Mattis stared at the demand without understanding.

Hege was so drunk with joy she didn't know what she was saying any longer, that was the trouble.

He still hadn't pushed the boat out—and in the event he never did, for he heard a faint rumbling in the air.

Thunder.

A bank of cloud was rising over the hills. At the same time there was a rumble from somewhere.

Well, there's only one thing to do now, he said. I never agreed to ferry anyone in a thunderstorm. Thank God I made that an exception.

He used an extra piece of rope to tie the boat up, in case the wind got really strong, put the oars under cover, and was off to his usual hiding place with no other thoughts in his mind. He didn't feel bound by normal agreements during thunderstorms. Half-way up the slope he suddenly remembered Hege's insistent demand: be grown-up! He stopped and thought about it.

Up at the top he saw Jørgen going into the house. Had he had an accident in the forest? Didn't look like it. Jørgen hadn't gone to the forest yet, was at home with Hege when he should be at work.

Things are in a real mess, Mattis thought. Jørgen doesn't fell trees and Hege doesn't knit sweaters. I'll soon be the only one here who does any work.

The rumbling was growing louder, and he walked faster. Suppose he went into the house and stayed with Hege and Jørgen while the storm was raging. Wouldn't that be a grown-up thing to do?

No, I daren't, he admitted. And he made straight for the usual, safe place. Maybe the storm wouldn't be as bad as last time, but it would be enough to sap him of all his strength. He got inside, fastened the door and put his fingers in his ears.

The storm wasn't any too light. Outside the thunder crashed, and the uncanny hissing sound started. Mattis sat huddled up. Not for a moment did it occur to him to act like a grown-up: the situation was far too serious.

But this time his hiding-place failed to give him proper protection. Neither the thunder nor the noise of his fingers in his ears could drown Jørgen's shout. It came from just on the other side of the wall. It was a stern voice full of authority.

'Mattis! Out you come!'

Out? Is he mad? thought Mattis. He didn't stir, just looked to make sure the hook was on the door.

Outside, the order was repeated.

'Come out, Mattis!'

It suddenly struck Mattis that this was just the way he'd called Jørgen down from the attic himself that day.

Jørgen shouted: 'Do I have to come in and *drag* you out! Out with you now, Mattis!'

What was going on? Jørgen was almost unrecognizable. Drag you out, he said, making it impossible to stay. Outside the thunder was crashing so violently that Mattis's face turned pale and his legs felt limp, but he had to go out now all the same—or there'd be nothing left of him. And all because it was Jørgen who stood there calling.

'I'm coming!' he shouted through the door.

He undid the hook and was almost blinded by a flash of lightning as he opened the door, it seemed to get right inside him—but he walked across the threshold and out on to the grass. There was a crash of thunder overhead. The rain had held off so far.

He hardly realized where he was—but there was Jørgen, standing right in front of him. Mattis was half-blinded, he saw Jørgen through a mist, and farther away he could just make out Hege standing in the doorway. She was gesticulating and waving to Jørgen, looked as though she was trying to make him stop—wanted Mattis to be spared this ordeal.

'Here I am!' Mattis announced simply, and stepped forward. All feeling had gone from his legs. He walked straight towards Jørgen who had stepped back a little. The lightning flashed again.

'What is it you want, Jørgen?'

Jørgen stood waiting, motionless and silent.

Mattis walked through lightning and thunder. He didn't collapse like an empty bag, didn't have his fingers in his ears, kept his eyes wide open, walked purposefully towards Jørgen—he'd show him!

He came up to him, and Jørgen received him, motionless as before.

'Good,' was all he said.

Jørgen said it with emphasis—Mattis could feel it. He said it with respect.

Mattis was trembling, but his legs carried him without giving way. He looked at Jørgen, with feelings of friendship and fear.

'Yes, but what is it?' said Mattis, in a frenzy of excitement. 'Tell me what you want with me?'

'Come in and sit with us,' said Jørgen, 'that's all. This is no place for you to stay.'

Mattis felt anger stirring inside him but he didn't dare to be angry in this kind of weather. He hesitated a bit, but finally followed him in. His heart was beating wildly. The worst part of the storm was over, the noise of the thunder was dying away.

Hege was still standing in the doorway, it was obvious she was uneasy about Mattis.

'I think you'd better let us come in,' Jørgen said to her.

Hege nodded, didn't know what to say. She followed them in, so that they were all together inside. Mattis stared helplessly at these strong and clever people. Yet he couldn't bring himself to sit with them, couldn't bring himself to do anything—the reaction was setting in after all the excitement. While the storm was subsiding he went over to his bench and lay down, dropped off into an easy slumber, his thoughts far away.

179

34

After this episode Mattis waited for something more from Jørgen. Expected him to call upon him to do other things as well. You never could tell what people like Jørgen might get up to.

Deep down inside Mattis was grateful to him for what had happened during the thunderstorm. For a brief moment he'd been a tiny little bit grown-up. But apart from this he was as bewildered as before, and full of misgivings. He noticed how happy Hege and Jørgen were together. The way Hege's face lit up with joy when Jørgen came home from the forest. Saw many small indications of the gap that now separated Hege from her old life, and from her brother.

What's going to become of me?

He kept an eye on them :

Do they think I can manage on my own?

I don't suppose they ever give it a thought.

He asked Hege straight out : 'Why did Jørgen drag me out into the thunderstorm?'

'He wanted to see how much you could take,' Hege replied. 'And it was more than we thought.'

Her words made him shudder. See if I could take it? He was pleased he'd passed the test. And this was probably only a foretaste of what Jørgen had in store for him.

A prey to worry and wild assumptions, he rowed around on the lake. There were no passengers; now and then a motor-boat went chugging past, and occasionally made straight for the hills in the west. No one wanted Mattis's ferry.

The only good thing is that I'm learning from Jørgen what to do when I meet girls, he thought. What a lot of things I didn't know. Surprising I managed as well as I did with Anna and Inger.

Those heavenly names always seemed so near out here on the water. He rowed slowly, and the boat went this way and that.

Before long Mattis was asking for decisions again: 'Do you know anything more now?' he asked Hege, in a tone that was almost unfriendly. There was no doubt what he was referring to.

'No,' Hege replied light-heartedly, 'we don't know anything. We're just happy. Why can't you be happy, too?'

She was a different person, seemed to have forgotten the past. When Mattis was near her, he saw how full of happiness she was—in a way he was able to share in her happiness. He could appear cheerful and bold, even devil-may-care: 'You might just as well tell me,' he said.

'Tell you what?'

'I can take it,' he said mysteriously, although deep down inside he was trembling with fear.

Hege looked at him hesitantly. She was blind, couldn't see. Then her happiness returned again, and she wanted to be off.

'Do you remember what things were like *before*?' he began, but he couldn't go on, had to leave without another word. Too many memories came back to him.

35

One morning Jørgen came towards him. He obviously had
something special in view. Mattis gave a start: this must
be some new test. Jørgen was probably going to carry on
where he left off. It was on a cool morning, at the beginning of September, with patches of mist drifting over the
lake, and blue sky overhead.

Jørgen had got ready to leave for the forest as usual,
now he came up to Mattis: 'You must come and work
with me in the forest for a bit now.'

'Got the ferry to look after,' Mattis replied curtly.

'No one to ferry now the autumn's here,' said Jørgen.
'You can come with me to the forest today.'

It sounded almost like an order, *that's* the sort of person Jørgen was. Mattis called Hege, and Hege appeared
at once.

'Am I supposed to go to the forest with Jørgen?'

'Yes, you go along with Jørgen,' she said. 'If you don't
know about felling trees, he'll teach you. I'll get some
sandwiches ready straight away.'

Mattis stood feeling lost.

Sandwiches were no longer a problem. They had plenty
to eat with the lumberjack there, compared with what
things had been like before. Mattis allowed himself to be
fitted out, but he didn't feel very happy about it.

'Good,' said Jørgen, when everything was done.

'What's the point of all this?'

'You're going to learn how to fell trees.'

It reminded him of the time when he'd been called out
into the thunderstorm. And now, just as he was getting

on so well with the ferrying and had got a steady job he could cope with.

On their way to the forest they walked through the village. People saw Mattis and the lumberjack walking together, and Mattis dressed like a lumberjack himself. It was nice, though it didn't mean as much now as it would have done earlier, in the spring. A lot of changes had taken place during the summer.

He had to laugh.

'Well?' said Jørgen, smiling.

'Oh nothing, I just remembered the way I couldn't thin out turnips in the spring.'

'Hm,' said Jørgen. He was a newcomer and didn't quite understand.

Mattis noticed this.

'The rocky island,' he said.

'I'm afraid I don't know what that means,' said Jørgen honestly.

'No, I suppose not,' said Mattis.

No further explanation was forthcoming, either.

They came to the spot where Jørgen had been felling trees. The place looked like a battlefield : there were tree-trunks everywhere, lying among severed branches. Mattis was plonked down by a half finished trunk and told to get the bark off. Jørgen set to on his own a little farther away.

Mattis did everything as best he could, but this was different from sitting in the boat rowing—here in the forest his thoughts got confused at once. And this showed on the tree-trunk, it began to look as if something had been gnawing at it. Over by Jørgen trees were crashing and branches snapping, and the ground trembled.

Mattis was sweating. Finally he announced that he'd finished.

Jørgen came over. Gave a kind of grunt. Apart from

that he didn't seem to be dissatisfied. The trunk must have looked awful to a real lumberjack.

'You take a little rest,' was all Jørgen said, 'and I'll add a few finishing touches here and there.'

Mattis sat down. Jørgen seemed to swallow the trunk with his barking iron, it was so small. A question was going round and round in Mattis's head : What am I here for?

'What am I here for?' he said aloud.

'To learn,' said Jørgen.

'Yes, but why?'

'It's a useful thing to be able to do, fell trees.'

Jørgen refused to explain any further. Mattis thought : it's all because they're going to leave.

'You called me out into the thunderstorm, too.'

'Yes, and you managed very well. Now we'll have a bite to eat, and rest for a bit.'

He handed Mattis the food.

'That wasn't what I—'

'No, but take it. You haven't had too much of it in your life.'

It was a sort of small token of friendship on Jørgen's part, but Mattis couldn't bring himself to touch what he'd been offered.

'You've brought me here for a reason !'

Jørgen was slowly chewing his sandwiches.

'It's your good we've got at heart,' he said, 'I can promise you that, Mattis.'

He ate a whole sandwich before saying anything more.

'We just don't know what to do,' he said suddenly and looked openly at Mattis.

'About me?' Mattis asked, quick on the uptake.

'Yes, of course.'

The big lumberjack sat chewing Hege's sandwiches. There was a kind expression on his face. In *one* way

184

Mattis wasn't afraid of him, but at the same time the things that Jørgen knew about and wouldn't tell him made him tremble.

'But we can talk about this later,' said Jørgen. 'You're going to learn how to fell trees now. People can earn money when they know how to do that, and then they can manage.'

'I manage all right,' Mattis blurted out.

'Oh yes, but it's best to be able to manage on one's own,' said Jørgen in a friendly but firm voice.

In the alert and watchful state of mind Mattis was in these days this could only mean one thing : they were going to leave him, there was no doubt.

'I don't want to learn !' he cried.

'Sometimes we have to do things we don't like,' said Jørgen, and it was the same voice that had summoned Mattis out into the thunder and lightning.

Mattis was going to have to give in. But suddenly he had an idea. He asked abruptly : 'Can I go home?'

Jørgen was facing the other way; all he did was make a slight movement with his back, but it was answer enough.

Mattis was entranced by his plan, it was a lightning plan.

'That was stupid of you !' he said to Jørgen.

Then he rushed off.

36

Hege saw her brother come running towards the house. She dropped everything she had in her hands and went rushing out to meet him, through the fence and over towards him, among the heather-covered humps :

'Has he hurt himself?'

'Who?'

'*Who?*'

'No, he's felling trees like mad.'

'Thank God for that,' said Hege, a smile of relief spreading across her face. 'The way you were coming along, it looked as if it was a matter of life and death, you know. You must never come rushing out of the forest like that when people are felling trees, or everyone'll think there's been an accident.'

'I forgot,' Mattis replied meekly, 'I was busy thinking about something else.'

'What is it then? Something to do with you?'

'Well, not really. I can't tell you *beforehand*.'

Mattis felt how clumsily he'd put this.

'I ran home because I've got to talk to you, and see you.'

Hege snorted: 'See me. Really, what will you think of next! Fancy frightening me like that, I thought he'd hurt himself.'

This was about as awkward a beginning for Mattis and his lightning plan as could possibly be imagined. Fancy tearing home in that stupid way—and when he'd been so sure he could win Hege back before Jørgen returned from the forest. In a flash he had seen a solution. But now? Hege was almost light-headed with happiness and relief about Jørgen—just because he hadn't hurt himself.

All the same it was Hege who finally started him off, as they stood there on the other side of the fence. Mattis was breathing heavily after the effort of running—and in a burst of joy Hege put her arm round him and pulled him down beside her on to a little hump.

'Sit down and get your breath back,' she said happily. 'You're sweating, too, after all that running.'

There they sat, side by side on the little hump—as if there were only the two of them, and nothing had changed.

And suddenly Mattis had a fresh idea; now he knew what to do :

First he smiled at her.

Hege smiled back, pleased.

Then he nodded.

She nodded back.

It was like an old forgotten game they'd suddenly re-discovered.

Mattis wasn't quite as innocent as she imagined now, he thought to himself. He had a plan.

'Here we are sitting on a hump,' he began.

Hege nodded. He went on : 'And we've sat on humps before.'

'Yes, we certainly have,' said Hege, 'not so very long ago either.'

Mattis laughed at his success. He must be clever now, and win Hege from Jørgen.

'There's nothing quite like sitting on humps with you.'

At this Hege looked at him, a little surprised; he had to hurry on : 'I think we ought to sit on humps much more often.'

'Oh?'

'What do you think, then?'

All Hege said was : 'Well, *you* can, can't you?'

He could see the barrier she was putting up between them. He was desperate and he wanted the truth.

'But not you?'

'Me? Well no,' said Hege. It was painful to see the way she was avoiding his gaze.

'Why not?'

'You know who I sit with,' she said.

She said it as simply as that, destroying his plan with

one blow. Now there was nothing left. It was as if all his ideas and enthusiasm were trickling away through a sieve. He'd lost almost before he'd begun.

'Well, that was all I wanted to talk about,' he said despondently and got up.

Hege didn't answer, wouldn't turn her face towards him, either. Mattis added: 'Strange the humps didn't help. And I thought I'd manage to win you back before Jørgen came home.'

Hege was still sitting on the soft hump. Now she got up, too, and said in a tone of despair: 'Well, I don't know.'

'What?'

'Don't you think we haven't talked about you?'

'I know jolly well you have,' said Mattis quickly.

'We'll do everything we can,' Hege said. 'You know we will, don't you?'

Mattis hardly noticed what she was saying. He saw her climb through the fence and go back inside. He was busy turning something over in his mind: lightning thoughts. What are lightning thoughts after all, when it comes to the point? Nothing. If you try and make use of them, they blow away like chaff, as soon as one of the clever ones opens his mouth. Hege only needs to say a word or two, and you've had it, the plan is in ruins.

Do everything we can, she said. She doesn't understand at all.

37

That was the end of the ferrying. It was impossible to escape from Jørgen's iron will. Jørgen took Mattis along to the forest every morning. You must learn, Jørgen said, in that brusque manner of his that made all protest impossible. Mattis protested, but went along all the same.

He returned, worn out after a difficult day, to the new kind of meal Hege was now providing.

'You must go through with this training,' she said.

It was no good trying to explain to her that your thoughts ran down neatly to the oars in a boat, but not to an axe or a barking iron—she just couldn't see it.

Jørgen was kind to him in the forest, it wasn't that. He picked out small trees for Mattis, easy to fell—and usually gave them a thorough going over afterwards. Mattis made no progress, he was dying to talk to Jørgen about Hege the whole time.

And he finally did, while they were having a rest and a cup of coffee. He had exhausted himself, but had little to show for it, had really only been turning the piles of branches. Now they were both lying on the ground, resting their heads on some stones, dozing fitfully, each one in his own world.

It was now or never.

Out into the storm! Mattis thought all of a sudden, to give himself courage. Then he sat up. Jørgen was wide awake at once, on his guard.

'Let's go on resting a bit longer, Mattis.'

'No, I want to talk to you!' Mattis announced, in the threatening tone in which this had to be said.

'Out with it.'

'Can't you see I'm finding it more difficult every day?'

It was true. He was getting worse rather than better. Jørgen knew this very well, that was why he couldn't bear to hear it, coming from Mattis.

'Yes, what's the matter with you?' he said, and for once his voice sounded irritable.

This gave Mattis the courage he needed. The angry tone.

189

'And what's the matter with *you*? Taking Hege away from me! What's the matter with a person like that?'

Jørgen was embarrassed.

'It's just the way things turned out,' was all he said.

They lay in silence. Hege was there, somewhere in between them, and didn't belong to either.

But then Jørgen said: 'Couldn't you think of Hege a bit as well? Doesn't *that* make you happy at all? What sort of a life d'you think she's had?'

Mattis was dumbfounded, needed time to see things from this new angle. Jørgen was probably right, but all the same. His thoughts flapped helplessly around while he remained sitting still. The world was full of forces you couldn't fight against which suddenly loomed up and aimed a crushing blow at you. It wasn't just Hege and Jørgen and all the other clever people—no, these forces were so powerful that he, Mattis, ferried his own misfortune across the lake, in his own boat, and asked it into his house. What could you do when things were like that?

'Well, shall we stop talking about this?' Jørgen suggested, since Mattis didn't answer.

Mattis said, frightened: 'I'm thinking nasty things about you now.'

'Tut-tut,' said Jørgen, 'that doesn't help much.'

'What does help, then?'

'We won't go on about this any more,' said Jørgen, harshly. 'Things are going to stay as they are.'

'Yes,' said Mattis. The nasty thoughts were still raging inside him, but he said yes and allowed himself to be shut up, lay down on the ground again.

They lay resting their backs. Jørgen had a little piece of stick in his hand, and in an absentminded way he aimed a blow at a couple of gleaming red toadstools close to him. The two men were resting in a clearing full of old branches and tree-stumps, tufts of grass and fat toadstools. Jørgen suddenly began talking about the beautiful toadstools in an effort to change the subject.

'Look at them, Mattis. If you ate those, it'd be the end of everything, I should think.'

The toadstools stood there, clothed in scarlet, split in two by Jørgen's stick. Their flesh was white and fresh, and contained poison and death.

Mattis gave a start, but remained lying with his eyes fixed on the toadstools.

'Do you really think so?'

'Yes, they're poisonous,' said Jørgen. 'In the old days they made them into broth when they wanted to go berserk and slaughter people.'

Mattis couldn't take his eyes off the toadstools, he was a prey to strange and frightening desires he was unable to control. Mattis looked at the toadstools and the toadstools looked back, took hold of him, seized control of his mind and body, bewitching him.

'Is that true?' he said.

'Yes, don't you touch them, or I'd get really frightened of you.'

'Don't say it,' said Mattis, but it was only a mumble. He stared fascinated at the toadstools, glanced quickly at Jørgen, and then went into action. It came to him all of a sudden, in the desperate plight he was in : I'll eat some! Eat some, whatever he says. Eat some.

His hand was already reaching down to get hold of a mouthful of the devilish poison.

'Stop it!' said Jørgen. 'It's really poisonous. Have you taken leave of your—'

Too late. Mattis was quicker, grabbed a piece of white flesh with scarlet skin round it, and stuffed it into his mouth. He didn't stop to think what it tasted like, swallowed it with a mighty gulp. His throat felt as if it was on fire—although it wasn't at all really. But at once it began to smart, so this was no ordinary food—and he uttered a short, sharp cry as well, like the angry snap of a dog.

'What are you trying to do, you fool!' said Jørgen.

Jørgen got really angry.

'Bring it up again!' he shouted. 'Stick your finger down your throat.'

'Too late,' said Mattis, half choked. His whole body felt different; it was part excitement and part imagination.

'Was it a large piece? Answer me! Are you that far gone already?'

Jørgen was furious.

Mattis just rolled his eyes around and tried to see if he was going berserk. He was afraid, his throat felt as if it was burning. The whole of my inside'll burn up soon, he suddenly thought, I must hurry.

He didn't let Jørgen out of his sight. With the toadstool swelling inside him, he watched his every movement, ready to act.

Jørgen was angry, and scared too. Didn't know how much of the toadstool Mattis had eaten. Could be it was really serious? He seized the grimy coffee-pot they used in the forest from the dying embers on which it had been standing, shook it and managed to squeeze out a cup of really strong lumberjack's coffee which he held out to Mattis: 'Here! Drink this.'

'Some hopes!' jeered Mattis, giving the cup a push and spilling everything. He was horrified at the way he was defying Jørgen, but proud, too. Defying Jørgen's will. After all, he'd been eating toadstools! Now Jørgen was for it himself—in his madness Mattis took aim.

When the cup fell from Jørgen's hand his face froze. He grabbed Mattis's wrist, and the aim came to nothing. His hand felt numb in the iron grip of the lumberjack.

'Are you mad already?'

Mattis rolled his eyes round.

'Let go!'

And Jørgen let go, but not because Mattis told him to. He seized the cup again and filled it with water from the little stream close by.

'Drink! Go on. Drink! Stick your finger down your throat, bring it up again!'

'Want to keep what I've got,' Mattis replied in an unrecognizable voice. Imagined his body was being slowly consumed by flames. And he had no wish to put the fire out, he was going to crush Jørgen completely! He felt his strength and wisdom growing apace.

Then Jørgen suddenly changed his tactics.

'All right, if that's the way you want it, then,' he said. 'I don't think you need worry anyway, a tiny little bit of toadstool like that isn't going to kill you. There wasn't enough of it. Sit down and behave like a normal human being again.'

'What?' said Mattis in a grating voice.

But oddly enough he did as he was told. Sat down, drank some of the water, too, but like a man in a dream. Yes, now he really *was* different. Wanted to be different. Had eaten dangerous things.

Yes, how different he felt, in mind and body, light and airy, somehow. He was both here and not here. He sailed above the tree-tops with the greatest ease. The first thing he thought of, quite automatically, was the woodcock.

'You sit down, too, Jørgen!' he said, wide-eyed and staring, 'and I'll tell you about the woodcock that got his wing full of lead and is lying under the stone. Why's he lying there?'

Jørgen growled: 'Full of lead! Full of crazy nonsense, you mean. You'd better go home.'

Mattis simply braced himself for more: 'Sit down, I

tell you. You're going to listen to me now. Yes, my turn had to come sooner or later.'

Jørgen sat down patiently.

'All right, tell me then.'

'I suppose Hege's already told you about the wood-cock?' said Mattis sternly.

'We've had so much to talk about, I can't remember whether I've heard about it or not.'

Mattis looked at him in disbelief.

'Can she possibly have anything more important to talk about than my woodcock?'

'Yes.'

'Didn't she say that the woodcock got shot, either?'

'Oh, perhaps she did, I don't remember. What is it that's so wonderful about this woodcock then?'

Mattis fixed Jørgen with a wild stare. He hadn't eaten toadstools for nothing : 'It was the woodcock and me, you see ! And now he's lying under the stone—but that doesn't make any difference, he's flying over the house, sort of, *sort of*, d'you see ! Me and the woodcock, sort of. We fly across here, sort of. We'll fly across here the whole time ! Just you try—'

He stopped, frightened.

'You and the woodcock. Of course, yes, you and the woodcock,' Jørgen murmured cautiously, on his guard.

'What are you saying that for?' Mattis interrupted. He still felt different; it was as though there was a blazing bonfire inside him.

'There's only Hege and you inside then, you see !' he said sternly to Jørgen, 'and it's not easy then, you see. It makes no difference what's lying under the stone or what isn't lying under the stone. Then.'

'Yes,' said Jørgen.

'What are you saying yes to?'

Jørgen was confused.

194

'No,' he answered.

Still staring at him, Mattis said: 'Can I ask you about something I haven't dared to ask about before, Jørgen?'

Jørgen indicated that he could.

'Me and the woodcock, sort of! That's the whole thing. Don't you understand anything?'

Jørgen shook his head.

Mattis was wandering along unknown paths. Felt something coming. What was it? No, it was coming, that was all. Crazy. Fire. Destruction. His eyes were burning, he fixed them on Jørgen, and at once Jørgen was consumed by flames. Serve him right.

Nonsense. I've been eating toadstools—that's what it is. But I'm *going to* cast the evil eye on Jørgen. Now I cast it on—

At once a dark shadow rose up and reached out for Jørgen. Nonsense again, it's only the toadstools I've eaten. I'm not dying. *Jørgen's* going to die!

The next moment he was fighting with Jørgen. Had sprung on him like a beast of prey and had him in his grip.

'Oh, you're out to get me, are you?' said Jørgen, in a cool, calm voice, brushing him aside. He held Mattis like a child.

'For heaven's sake pull yourself together, you fool.'

Jørgen picked Mattis up and carried him a few paces over to the stream. There he started pouring water on to his distorted face. To begin with Mattis struggled, but the water, autumn cold, quenched the fire inside him. He quietened down, recovered his senses. And immediately he collapsed, groaned with shame and remorse.

'I didn't want to kill you!'

'No, that's not so easy,' said Jørgen.

'Where's Hege? She's not dead?'

Jørgen almost jumped: 'Shut up! What a load of rubbish you're talking I'm not going to have any more of this nonsense, d'you understand?'

It sounded as though it was Jørgen's axe talking, it was so stern and sharp.

Mattis's head was gradually clearing. Still confused he said : 'What have I been doing?'

'You've been imagining things. Eating toadstools and playing the fool.'

'Doesn't matter, as long as you're still alive,' said Mattis, overjoyed all of a sudden.

Jørgen was easily embarrassed by this sort of thing.

'All right, all right—'

A complete change came over Mattis now, his excitement took a different turn, he began to think of pleasant things, and wanted to tell Jørgen—he was so grateful for the fact that Jørgen was alive and that he hadn't killed him while he'd been bewitched by the toadstools.

'Anna and Inger,' he said out of sheer gratitude, placing the names in Jørgen's hands like a gift. 'Have you any idea what *that* is?'

Jørgen didn't answer, just waited.

'Have I told you about them before, Jørgen?'

'No. Who are they?'

'Girls,' said Mattis proudly.

'Yes, I gathered that.'

'I rowed them. Last summer. We were on a rocky little island. The whole village stood watching as we landed by the store.'

'Well, that'll teach them a thing or two,' said Jørgen.

Mattis closed his eyes in wonderment; Jørgen had hit on just the right answer. Here was a person who knew the sort of things that were important for a man.

'Can I ask you something, Jørgen?' he therefore began.

'You were asking something a moment ago, too. And I didn't understand a thing. But go on.'

'What I want to know is,' said Mattis, hesitating a little, 'whether you think about girls during the middle of the week?'

It caught Jørgen by surprise, but he answered without batting an eyelid:

'Yes, I'm sure I do.'

'Have you ever?'

'Yes, I'm sure.'

'Oh well,' said Mattis, sighing with relief, 'that's all right then.

'Yes, it's odd, isn't it,' he went on, looking up, free from all murderous desires.

'What is?'

'Oh, I don't know—lots of things.'

'No, we've wasted enough time now,' said Jørgen all of a sudden, and started felling trees with mighty blows.

Mattis stayed sitting there; his mood was an odd mixture of happiness and shock at the way he'd behaved. He trampled the remains of the toadstools to bits with his boots. Then he laughed with joy. I've been imagining things, he said, using the words of his stern boss.

38

But the episode made a deep impression on Mattis all the same. When the first wave of relief had subsided, he was left with a feeling of horror that refused to go away.

I almost killed Jørgen—how could I have done a thing like that?

Or was it just because of the toadstool I ate?

He followed Hege around for a day or two, expecting

to get the telling off he'd deserved. Hege said nothing, and in the end he had to take the initiative himself.

'Hasn't Jørgen said anything?'

'What about?'

'About me and him, and that sort of thing—in the forest, about eating toadstools and that sort of thing.'

'No, had you expected him to?'

'No.'

'Has anything happened?' Hege asked.

'No, it never came to anything, can't you see that?'

Mattis drifted away. Was surprised at Jørgen.

Jørgen had called him to come along to the forest the following day as well, but Mattis answered: 'I'm not going there again!'

He sounded so terrified that Jørgen left it at that. Having Mattis in the forest had been nothing but a nuisance to Jørgen anyway, so he was probably past caring.

Mattis stayed sitting on the bench, looking out of the window. Hege hovered uneasily around him. There was no doubt she'd asked Jørgen all about what had happened and he'd told her. Now she approached her brother and said, feeling her way: 'Better start ferrying again, Mattis.'

'P'raps.'

'But you were so happy doing it.'

'It may be diffierent now,' said Mattis.

'Oh well.'

Hege was on the move again. She was always on the move nowadays, particularly when her sweetheart was around. She did the housework with swift hands, was blossoming with new life. Mattis was well aware of the changes in her. All he could do was repeat the same tiring question, the one he asked every day: 'What's going to become of *me*?'

He didn't start ferrying again. Something had changed. He roamed idly about, gave a start when he noticed a gleaming red object by the fence. There stood a huge toadstool, full of ugly, hidden fury. Was standing right next to the fence, as if it were trying to peep in at Mattis.

No no, he thought, frightened, fighting against it. I'll crush it before it casts its spell on me.

He walked across and gave the toadstool a kick. It disintegrated in a blaze of red and white.

A little later he found another one, inside the fence, on their own land. Just as beautiful. He didn't kick it this time, just withdrew, feeling hot and prickly. He knew the whole place was full of them now, all the slopes and the forest floor, and over by the fence and in among the humps.

The house was surrounded by poison.

Had it been like this in previous years? He'd never noticed. Where did they come from? They seemed to grow larger while you stood watching them.

He thought clearly and distinctly: Jørgen may die in amongst all this, he's the one who's surrounded.

No, no! I don't want him to!

But the thought came creeping back, like a footless beast. What am I going to do, he said horrified, unable to move.

I *must* do something. It won't be long before I go for him again.

In the end he did what he always did: turned to the clever ones. Went to Hege as usual.

'Aren't there more red toadstools than usual this year?' he asked without explanation.

'Not as far as I can see,' said Hege. 'Everything's the same as always,' she said, understanding nothing. Was already on the move again.

39

And as a sign that no one was surrounded by poison a girl came walking down the path.

At first Mattis couldn't believe his eyes. He even knew her: it was the girl he'd worked with in the turnip field last spring. The one who had pinched her boy-friend so delightfully, and got pinched herself in the same blissful and delightful way. It was like a miracle, seeing her coming down from the road at a moment as gloomy as this.

It's me she's come to see, Mattis thought at once, remembering what had happened on the island in the lake.

Oh, but I'm forgetting, she's got a sweetheart.

It was years and years since a girl had come to visit them. Hege was the only one here. As soon as he saw her coming he thought: Anna or Inger? But when she got closer he saw it wasn't either of them. That would have been too good to be true, anyway. He was happy as it was, he knew this girl as well.

The fact that they'd worked together on one occasion gave Mattis confidence and put him at his ease. That's the sort of girl she'd been, he remembered. Looked as if they both remembered it, for the girl nodded as though she knew him, and smiled. All Mattis's misery vanished, the forest was no longer full of poison, it was like a friendly shield.

Before the girl had had a chance to say a word—almost before she'd reached him, Mattis blurted out: 'Aren't you sweethearts any longer?'

The girl laughed.

'Who?'

'You and him, of course. The chap who was pinching your arms and legs.'

'How can you tell, then?' she asked. 'People don't go rol. d holding hands the whole time, you know.'

Mattis bent his head. Had he said something stupid already? Thinking about it, she was right of course. The girl put an end to his embarrassment by saying: 'But actually, you're right. It's all over between us.'

Mattis felt a pang. Or rather two pangs: one of pleasure and one of sorrow.

'Surely there's no need for you to look so dismayed, is there?' said the girl.

'No,' he mumbled.

'No, that sort of thing doesn't always last. I expect you know that yourself,' she added comfortingly. A kind-hearted girl.

He didn't dare tell her an outright lie with a straight-forward 'yes', he turned it into an ambiguous 'hm' instead. But how grateful he was.

'Is there anyone at the moment, then?' he asked nerv-ously. 'Anyone new?'

'No, I'm more or less free at the moment,' said the girl with a careless toss of the head.

'Oh,' said Mattis.

The girl laughed again, for no apparent reason, but it wasn't a malicious laugh. Then at last she was able to get round to the subject of her visit.

'I've got a message to give to the lumberjack you've got living here, Jørgen something or other, isn't it? But I don't suppose he's home at this time of day.'

'No, he's out in the forest,' Mattis answered a little crossly. It looked as though he'd been wrong, it was Jørgen she wanted to see.

'But maybe I could tell you instead. You're capable of

giving a message, aren't you?' she blurted out without thinking.

Mattis went a bit red. But the girl was too young and gay and full of her own concerns to notice.

Mattis didn't dare take the message. He might get it wrong. Especially as it concerned Jørgen.

'It'd be better if you left it with my sister, if you don't mind. She's in there,' he said. It was a bitter thing to have to say.

The girl grinned.

'Of course. I forgot.'

She tripped in on nimble feet. Mattis followed her with his eyes, and had already forgiven her. He'd become a changed person after last summer—after rowing with Anna and Inger, and walking through the thunderstorm, and managing so well as ferryman. It wasn't difficult to forgive this girl for saying things she oughtn't to say.

And this was why sudden plans were flickering through his mind, too; plans concerning the visitor and another chance to talk to her. He walked up the path until he was hidden from the cottage, and there he stopped and waited. The girl would have to pass by here on her way home.

It worked like a charm. After a little while she came up the path and walked straight into him—rather like falling into a trap. But she did so with a carefree laugh.

'So that's where you are. Lying in wait for me on my way home.'

Funny how the clever ones saw through everything straight away. Or nearly everything. He couldn't use the same carefree tone as she had, the problems he was grappling with were far too difficult for that, far too grave, really. He stepped forward and asked in a serious voice : 'Can I come with you for a bit of the way? Just up to the road?'

"Course you can,' said the girl. Just like that.

'Yes, I thought it'd be all right, seeing you haven't got a sweetheart,' Mattis stammered.

'I didn't say that,' said the girl, 'I said I was *more or less* free. Oh yes, I've got one. Sort of, anyway.'

Mattis's eyes opened wide, and he slowed down. His face fell. He didn't understand.

'Don't you want to come then?' she said. 'Oh well, just as you like.'

'Want to?' He didn't understand. How could he walk with her, if she *had* a sweetheart after all? What was the point?

She wanted to go, but a movement of his arm stopped her. It was the sort of movement people make when they're trying to catch something, but then decided to let it fall.

There was a big flat stone by the side of the path. Mattis had walked past it all his life without noticing it— but today it seemed to detach itself from its surroundings. Mattis felt he ought to go, but there this stone was—and without knowing how he'd managed to think of it so quickly, he pointed to it and said hastily: *'Flat stones are for sitting on.'*

The way he said it made the girl sit down at once. Before he had time to think.

This is mad, he thought, and sat down next to her.

There was plenty of room on the stone. Mattis took good care not to get too near her. What did he want? Couldn't say for sure. To hear something. Be near. But he mustn't sit there without saying a word, he realized that. The girl seemed to be looking at him expectantly, insisting he say something. And so, rather abruptly, he asked: 'Did you think that was cleverly put?'

The girl was stroking her cheek with a blade of grass. Jerking her foot up and down. Never quite relaxed.

'What d'you mean?'

203

'What I said about the flat stone, of course. And about sitting.'

The girl snorted, was back on her feet already.

'Do you ask *that* sort of question, too?' she said, disappointed, as if she had had enough of him.

Had enough of him—

'But how—?' he asked, frightened. Stayed sitting on the stone.

The girl was going, and Mattis didn't dare to move.

'Didn't know it was wrong,' he said.

'No, well, I'm sorry I can't stay any longer.'

'You see—'

She interrupted him: 'Let's not go on about it. It's not important; doesn't matter to either of us, does it?'

She started to walk away. She nodded first, in a friendly way, perhaps a little ashamed. But she was going.

Mattis clung to a memory: 'The others weren't like that!' he said. 'And I talked to them a lot.'

The girl stopped at once.

'The others? Who are they?'

'I mean Anna and Inger, when I say the others,' he said in a low voice. 'You've heard about them, haven't you?'

'Yes I—of course I have.'

'We were out on the lake, and we talked together for a whole day. And they weren't like that.'

The girl came towards him, looked straight into his eyes, regretting what she'd said. His eyes opened wide. What was he expecting? He didn't know. But he waited.

'Listen, Mattis.'

He was trembling.

'Yes?'

She didn't know what to say. She'd looked into his eyes.

'No, I—' she began. 'Oh, it's impossible to know *what* to say to you!'

As she spoke, she brushed his cheek lightly with her

204

hand, and then she really did go, quick, nimble, gone in a trice.

Mattis didn't try to pinpoint his feelings, but everything had been set right, and more besides. On a happy impulse the girl had done what neither Anna nor Inger had done —and had gained a place in his heart.

He remained sitting on the stone for a long time.

40

Then it came. Something quite different: the lightning flash that solved his problems. Suddenly and without warning he saw it all. And it was difficult.

He jumped up from the flat stone.

Like a blinding flash of lightning. But it was inside him this time, lit up everything.

What! he thought, horrified. I can't do it.

He forgot the girl. He'd been sitting thinking happily about the wonderful moments she'd given him—and then came the flash. *A way out*, ready and complete from beginning to end—in a flash.

Suddenly and ruthlessly it cut through the problems that had been gathering around him. He had to accept it without question, without fear—although its effect was shattering. He saw what he had to do, understood it and accepted it, numbly.

And that was how his plan came—in a flash while he was sitting on the stone, the stone now so dear to him after what had just happened. The way out of the difficulties that had been tormenting him. Hege and Jørgen and me, he thought. The woodcock wasn't included this time, it was somewhere else.

He sat down again without thinking.

'This is going to be difficult,' he said in a loud voice into the empty air. But nobody was listening. How painful it had proved, becoming one of the clever ones.

41

The plan was secret. Everything had to be done with the utmost caution. He couldn't even mention it to Hege— she'd have intervened at once and stopped him.

But since it was a difficult plan, he must allow himself one last attempt to get off more lightly, he felt, now that the first flash of excitement had died down.

So he waited till Jørgen had left for the forest the next day, and then approached Hege in a somewhat ceremonious manner. She was sitting among her sweaters, humming a little tune.

'What is it, Mattis?' she said and stopped humming. It was obvious from his appearance that he had something serious on his mind.

'It's important,' he answered, 'more important than you realize.'

'Well, come on then, tell me,' said Hege, a bit impatiently.

Mattis's throat sounded dry: 'You must decide who you want to be with from now on, Jørgen or me,' he said, plunging straight in.

Hege didn't need any explanation. She didn't need to think about it, either, as far as he could see.

'Nothing's changed, as far as I'm concerned,' she said without hesitation. 'Surely you realize who I'm going to be with—from now on.'

'Yes,' said Mattis in a faltering voice, 'but then it's going to be—' He broke off, had nearly said too much.

Hege tackled the problem from her angle: 'Doesn't it strike you as natural, too, if you really think about it?'

Thinking about it, he had to admit she was right. But all the same. And things might change. He clung to this faint hope. I've heard they can. These things can come to nothing. That's what happened to the two who were pinching each other.

He staked a lot on his next question: 'And are you sure things won't ever change, Hege?'

'As sure as I'm sitting here,' Hege replied. 'And thank God for that.'

Mattis bent his head.

'Oh well, in that case.'

Hege obviously knew what she was talking about. She sounded absolutely certain. There was no hope of winning her back.

'This is clever and difficult,' he said. 'It may not be easy to manage.'

'Manage what?' she asked, not understanding, 'don't you think Jørgen and I'll manage?'

He was dumbfounded. She didn't understand a thing. But then she clinched the matter by saying: 'You mustn't begrudge me this, Mattis.'

Slam. The door was shut.

'Begrudge,' he said.

His way was barred; there was nothing more he could say.

'Was there anything else you wanted?' Hege asked in a friendly tone, since Mattis remained standing there without saying anything.

Mattis shook his head. Hege had been as clear as you could wish. So now things were more or less settled. He'd have to get on with his big plan. He was just standing there for a while first.

42

For many years a couple of rough-hewn pieces of wood, that looked as though they might one day be oars, had been standing in the shed. Mattis had never got down to finishing them, he'd managed with the old ones. Now he brought out these half-finished oars, and started scraping at them with a plane.

The plan had caught his imagination so completely that he even saw these clumsy pieces of wood as part of it. Yes, my mind was really working well for once! he thought, with a strange sensation running through his body. He felt he was completely in the hands of the unknown.

Jørgen came back from the forest, and saw Mattis standing there scraping away with his plane. An unusual sight.

'Are you going to make a new pair of oars?'

'Yes, I've been meaning to for a long time,' said Mattis.

'You're going to start ferrying again, then?' said Jørgen, urging the idea on him.

'Suppose so.'

Mattis answered without looking up. He couldn't be entirely truthful now—or his plan would be spoilt, and altogether forbidden. Perhaps they'd tie him up.

'Good,' said Jørgen, 'it's a bad thing for anyone to be without a job.'

And he went in to join Hege and have his meal.

The oars were much too big and thick, but Mattis just scraped them to make them white and a little smoother, so they'd look more finished. They remained rough pieces of wood—and that was how they were going to be used. Supported by these oars he would either float and reach land in safety, or else sink beneath them and disappear. That was the most important part of the whole plan.

Then I'll know what I'm to do. I'll find out.

The boat's going to spring a leak, right in the middle of the lake, so it sinks to the bottom. It's so rotten it's bound to. And *I* don't know how to swim. But these thick oars should bear me up and bring me back—if I'm *meant* to come back and be with them again.

But it won't be my decision.

But it's difficult, he thought.

When the oars were finished and shining white, he went to bed. Now everything was ready, a strange feeling crept over him. Only one thing left to do.

But not tomorrow, he thought.

Why not? a voice seemed to ask, impatient and persistent.

Well, it's just the way things are, he answered. And that would have to do.

He was lying in his bench, looking up at the window. A faint light came in from the night outside.

Hege and Jørgen hadn't been about when he came in in the evening, but he had heard subdued voices coming from the attic. Happy voices most likely—saying the kind of things he longed so much to hear. But talking about him as well, no doubt, and not so happy then—they must feel he was a terrible burden, after all.

But now the oars are ready, so I'll soon know what's to happen.

He brushed the thought aside, didn't want to face it. A moment later he said to himself: I suppose it's no different from facing up to a thunderstorm.

Above him the voices were still murmuring away. There was a peal of laughter, too, which was stopped as abruptly as a marble rolling across the floor. So that was how Hege could laugh when she was happy. Hadn't he known this before?

But now they were probably talking about him again. There was no more laughter.

'Gosh, listen to that!' he said suddenly, in a loud and happy voice, sitting up in the bench.

A gust of wind outside.

A sudden autumn wind.

The house moaned softly as the wind penetrated its ramshackle old walls, and a sigh from afar ran through the trees; the waves would be getting up on the lake.

Wonderful.

He relaxed, filled with a sense of peace.

Now it's bound to be windy tomorrow. And that means I shan't be able to do anything. It's got to be calm when I row out. Now I can sleep.

He fell asleep at once; it had been a tense and tiring day.

43

A calm day, no wind on the water—these were the only conditions he had made. The lake must be like a mirror when he started his test, or it wouldn't count. Then it remained to be seen whether the wind would *come*.

It was an obvious condition, he thought.

The wind kept up for days on end.

The oars were ready and the boat was ready—and Mattis himself got up every morning with an uneasy, thumping heart : Was the lake smooth?

But every morning there was a wind. The tightness in his chest relaxed when he saw it.

One more day, he thought. And no one knows! Isn't it strange.

A little later he suddenly thought : That's the way it is with everything.

He ambled about. Jørgen made no further reference to the ferrying, nor did he ask Mattis to work in the forest.

The fiery red toadstools were still everywhere, but they didn't frighten Mattis now. They couldn't change anything.

And no one knows anything. Hege and Jørgen see a new pair of oars that are much too big, and don't realize a thing. They just think I can't make them any smaller.

Am I *really* clever now?

It's not a day too soon, he thought.

Another morning dawned. He was trying to brace himself against the shock of hearing Hege say to Jørgen out in the kitchen : 'The lake's like a mirror today.'

But it was likely to be a nasty moment, when it finally came.

He thought of other ways in which she might say it : 'Not a breath of wind today,' she could well say. 'So quiet there must be some reason for it,' she might say that, too.

Hege didn't say any of these things. No doubt she had more important matters to discuss with Jørgen than the weather. The weather didn't make much difference to either of them. Jørgen felled trees, come rain, come shine.

So the lake may be as calm as a millpond, even though Hege hasn't said anything, he thought as he lay in his bench. And when he got up his body felt twice its normal weight. He had to go out and see.

Thank God—

Still windy, the lake covered with dark-blue waves beneath a clear sky. It was strange looking at it, now it meant to much. Another day's delay.

While he was eating he noticed that Hege was watching him. He lost his appetite at once and went out. Does it show, after all? He got out some tools, reappeared in the doorway and said he was going down to mend the boat.

'That's right, you go and mend the boat,' said Hege pleased. 'Then I'll know where you are.'

'Yes, then you can sit by the window keeping an eye on me,' said Mattis provokingly.

'Why should I?'

'Well, don't you?'

He went off, fumbled around and patched up the boat a bit. At the same time he discovered a really rotten piece on the bottom, underneath the loose planks he was treading on. It wouldn't be difficult to send his foot crashing through it, if he gave it a really heavy kick. And he certainly felt he had enough strength at the moment, more than enough.

Flat stones are for sitting on, he mumbled as he worked. It *was* well put, but the girl hadn't appreciated it. Oh well, it doesn't worry me, nothing like that does.

He sat down beside the boat and turned his face towards the wind on the lake.

Blow, wind! was his secret wish.

There were far too many things to think about.

A stone over every eye, he said for no particular reason.

Anna and Inger and everything, he said.

Every tree where birds have been sitting, he said.

Every path where my sister Hege's been walking.

But it was too much for him, he didn't dare mention anything more.

The boat smelt of tar as usual, and of rotten planks warmed by the sun. Mattis looked at the lake; the wind was digging deep furrows on the surface, waves were gurgling at his feet.

But soon it was bound to be calm. A wind can never last. A calm can never last either. Me and the woodcock, sort of, he said disjointedly.

44

When nothing more could be done to the boat, he went back up to Hege.

'Is the boat all ready for ferrying now?' she asked, urging him on as Jørgen had done.

'Yes, everything's ready now. Tomorrow I'm going to begin ferrying like I did before,' said Mattis.

He didn't look at his sister.

'Tomorrow? Yes, of course,' said Hege decisively. 'Just the thing, Mattis.'

Down on the shore he'd been thinking out what to say. And the conversation was going just the way he wanted.

'That is, if the wind isn't too strong,' he went on. 'But the boat's completely rotten, so I daren't row out when it's windy any more. You could easily put your foot through the bottom, if you put it in the wrong place.'

It was hard to say this in a casual tone, but he managed somehow. Hege forgot her own concerns for a moment, and thought only of her brother's safety. She said: 'Then surely it's dangerous in calm weather, too, isn't it? In which case I don't think you ought to be allowed to use it.'

Mattis snorted.

'I know the boat all right.'

'Are you sure? I don't want you to sink to the bottom, you know.'

'Oh, nonsense.'

Inwardly he was in a state of turmoil as he carried out this stage of his plan. But everything worked satisfactorily, he said the right things, the things he realized it was safe to say, and he knew exactly what these were. Isn't it odd that you only become clever when it's too late? he thought.

'When it's calm I can stay out on the lake all day, for that matter,' he said. 'You don't need to worry, Hege, I know what I can and can't do. And where to put my foot and where not to put it.'

'Well, all right then, but just you be careful,' said Hege and hurried off. But a moment later she came back and said: 'I think I'll get Jørgen to decide after all—whether the boat's dangerous or not. Jørgen understands these things. If he says the boat's no good, you shan't use it any more.'

'Jørgen!' Mattis exclaimed.

This was one thing Jørgen must be kept out of, a moment that had nothing whatever to do with him. Mattis burst out wildly: 'I can manage without Jørgen! Everything! If you bring Jørgen into it, I'll do something dreadful!'

She stepped back.

'But Mattis—'

'Don't you dare fetch Jørgen! I'll tell him a thing or two if you do!'

'Now stop it,' said Hege. 'You don't need to tell Jørgen

anything. Jørgen's a good man, and he's done you no harm.'

But Mattis found it hard to stop: 'It depends on the weather now!' he said frantically.

'The weather?'

'Yes, d'you hear? The wind and the weather. Do you suppose I haven't been *thinking*?'

The word they normally avoided for Mattis's sake—and here he was using it himself, carefully and deliberately.

Hege gave way a little.

'I'm sure you've been thinking about a lot of things,' she said. 'We've all got a lot to think about, after what's happened.'

'After what's happened'—this was the only thing she seemed aware of. He stood in front of her, sad and dejected. She wasn't the same. She was a part of Jørgen. Half Jørgen.

'How could you become like this?' he asked.

'How do you mean?'

'Like—like you are, of course! I can hardly recognize you, the way you are now. What's the matter with you?'

'The matter with me? Well, you know. I've told you. I'm happy.'

The certainty of it washed through her like a wave.

'And once I hugged you for it, Mattis, don't you remember?'

It was as if Jørgen was standing beside her as she spoke, but in spite of this her words brought Mattis's violent outburst to an end. He could only say calmly: 'Go on up to Jørgen, then.'

Hege didn't look surprised.

'That's just where I'm going,' she said, and went.

Mattis was left sitting there. Outside he heard the friendly wind. Twilight fell. He began looking around in a special way. Didn't want to, but he couldn't help it. Up in the attic he could hear the endless murmur of Hege's and Jørgen's voices.

Now everything's ready, he thought. I managed to tell her about the boat rather well. Now let it blow or be calm, there's nothing more I can do.

After his sharp struggle with Hege and all the thinking he'd done that day he felt ready to drop, and he crawled into bed earlier than usual.

Up in the attic the talking had stopped—to Mattis's delight and sorrow. Outside, the wind was blowing and proclaiming its presence in a hundred different ways, affirming that it would blow tomorrow as well.

45

But now the wind has stopped.

Mattis woke up later that same night, and realized this almost before he was properly awake. The wind had stopped, hadn't told the truth. No rustle in the trees, no whisper. Mattis's first thought was : Not at night! I never said I was going to try at night.

Tomorrow morning it may be windy again, even if it's stopped now. The wind often dies down at night.

Bright moonlight shone through the window. A big new moon had appeared since the night he'd been rowing.

Once more he told himself that the wind dies down at night. But it was no good; the wind had stopped in a different way from before. Rubbish! How could you tell, lying in bed asleep?

There wasn't a sound in the house.

Is Hege in her own room? That's none of my business,

he told himself sternly. Surely it's enough for me that the wind's stopped.

He couldn't bear to go on lying there like this for long, he had to go out and have a look. He dressed quietly, in a hushed and silent house. Went.

The moonlight formed its usual streak across the water. And on the lake not a breath of air stirred. The lake was much broader than it had ever been before—Mattis looked at it spellbound.

He saw the forest too, and the grassland, and the stream with plants along its banks. Just to be able to drink from a stream, he suddenly thought.

He walked through the dew down to the little hollow where the stream ran. It was a tiny stream and said nothing to Mattis, but all the same there was a little pool in it.

Mattis didn't want to go down to the pool, didn't want to see his face in it, it felt so stiff and unnatural, and he was sure he'd be able to see it in the bright moonlight.

As he looked at the motionless lake, a clear voice inside him asked: How do you want things to turn out? It's not at all certain what'll happen in the boat, no one can tell.

He didn't want to think about it. Couldn't, even. With his face turned upwards, as if he were addressing the bright moon itself, he said in loud and stern tones: 'It's nothing to do with me any longer, it's in the hands of others. I've placed the whole thing in the hands of others.'

These were his words to the moon. Then he stumbled across the clearing, over to the fence and the humps, and towards much that was strange and inexpressible, just as it had always been. All my life, he thought suddenly, but pushed that aside, too. Keep off things like that!

Still, he sat down on one of the humps for a while. There were a lot of them, and they all looked kind and friendly, inviting him to stay there for a while. In the full light of the moon he seemed to become a lifeless being alongside his own shadow, part of a secret game moon and shadows were playing.

Before long he started shivering with cold, walked across the clearing and went in. Crawled back into bed. Sleep was impossible.

The depths, he thought. This was where his restless thoughts had finally led him. But there are so many : weedy depths, he thought. Sandy depths. Slime. Stony depths. Rocks and boulders. Depths no one has dreamt of.

But then there's this *other* thing, too, he thought confusedly, going as far as he dared. Then you rise up again through all the depths.

That's where I'm going in the end, surely? he asked dreamily, clinging to the thought.

Yes, that's where I'm going, he repeated.

He couldn't sleep. The wind stood still.

46

Mattis must have dropped off to sleep after all some time towards dawn. He hadn't noticed Hege walking past him on her way out to the kitchen. Hadn't even noticed Jørgen. They were both in the kitchen when Mattis woke up. He heard the clattering of cups—and then something that jolted him right out of his sleep : 'It's so quiet today, it's almost—'

It was addressed to Jørgen, just a casual remark, probably something said while she busied herself getting his sandwiches ready and poured him a cup of coffee.

'Yes, isn't it,' Jørgen answered indifferently.

'So he'll be able to get out on the lake today all right,' said Hege.

Mattis didn't hear whether Jørgen made any reply to this. He felt a shiver run right through his body. His thoughts swept over him from all sides, almost completely overcoming him. But he had to suppress them as best he could, managed to pull himself together and behave in a normal way.

Now you just stay where you are, he said to his thoughts, and got dressed. There was nothing left to do now except carry out the plan.

From the window he could see the lake. It was just as calm as when he'd been outside the night before. Nothing moved except a few thin veils of mist—it was a fine autumn morning. The sun hadn't risen yet, but it would soon appear in all its glory and burn away what odd patches of mist there were.

Mattis was still struggling violently with his thoughts when he came into the kitchen. Anyone could see that. Hege was there alone. Jørgen had already left, Mattis noted thankfully.

'What's the matter?' Hege asked at once. She saw it was no ordinary morning.

Mattis simply shook his head in reply.

'Tell me,' she demanded sternly, knowing her brother as she did, and up to a point he obeyed.

'I'm almost killing myself, I'm thinking so much,' he replied truthfully.

'Oh, is that all,' said Hege.

He gave a start.

'Come and have your breakfast,' she said.

He tried to swallow a few mouthfuls. His answer had satisfied Hege and she asked no further questions. Mattis followed her with his eyes, and at last he announced: 'Well, today the ferrying starts.'

219

Hege reacted with obvious pleasure.

'Yes, that's right, Mattis. That's a splendid idea.'

Had she been waiting all that eagerly? But then she remembered the dangerous boat.

'But actually—you once said the boat was a bit rotten. Is it still?'

'No, it's not too bad really.'

'Do have a good look at it, and if it's dangerous. . . .'

'Not when it's calm. It was when it's windy I meant.'

'Well, keep an eye on it,' she said, and was on the move. 'I won't cut any sandwiches for you today. You can come up when you feel hungry.'

'Yes,' said Mattis.

Now he was ready, had to go. He remained standing in the middle of the floor. In the end Hege asked: 'Anything you want?'

'No,' he said.

And with that he had to go. He could have said quite a few things now, but it wouldn't have been right. It was difficult to have to leave, with so much unsaid.

As he walked down the slope the sun rose above the ridge. There was a gentle autumn warmth in its rays that made the scenery translucent, made it somehow easy to walk among the shining foliage. And yet it was far from easy.

Mattis saw how the day was taking shape. The slope felt long and difficult, so he said in a loud and stubborn voice: 'It's going to be nice ferrying today.'

A few paces farther down he said: 'There may be a lot of people coming for the ferry today.'

Still farther down: 'And *that's* a good thing.'

With these thoughts he had managed to cover the length of the little path he was so fond of, down to the beach and the boat. The smell of tar struck him, called to life by the morning sun. The huge new oars were leaning against a clump of alders, their white wood shining. Mattis put them in the boat.

And now there's nothing more.

What about—?

No—

He'd have to act quickly now. Quickly out with the boat. He pushed it out. But then he looked around him, wildly, dragged the boat in again and rushed back over the pebbles up to the clumps of birch and alder which edged the curve of the shore so delicately and neatly. He ran right up to the light grey stem of an alder, and bit his teeth into the bark so that the bitter juice smarted. This was something nobody must see, and it lasted only a moment. And for that wild moment he remained standing there stiffly, then he tore a bit of the wood off and half ran back to the boat again—while the marks of his teeth started turning red in the trunk.

What now?

Nothing more.

He glided away from the shore. He was rowing and the things he was leaving behind remained in view the whole time.

47

There was nothing out on the lake, except for a motor-boat chugging along and growing smaller and smaller. There must be no one to interfere with what he had to do. It had been a great strain, tearing himself away just now —but all the same he managed to fix his thoughts on the right oar and the left oar in the usual way without getting into a muddle. Rowed as regularly as he would on any ordinary day. He didn't even fix his gaze on anything on the shore this time to keep a straight course, and yet he rowed straight out of sheer habit.

The bow pointed towards the desolate slopes in the west, but the oarsman had his back to them. As he got farther out he could see an ever greater expanse of shore from where he was sitting. Everything he saw seemed friendly and inviting.

From time to time he thought: Don't look at it.

But he couldn't stop himself from thinking. *One person's like this, another's like that,* he thought. That was as near as he dared come to thinking about it. He had to draw the line somewhere, if he were to have the strength to carry out his plan.

Only the decision's no longer mine, I've placed it in the hands of others.

The thick new oars lay across the stern, pointing towards land—they'd easily keep him afloat in calm weather, if the boat sank beneath him. He couldn't swim a single stroke, and now that was just as it should be—if he'd known how to, the test would have been meaningless.

He was assailed by all sorts of temptations—the clear autumn air and the yellowing trees. He beat them off, whatever shape they took.

Far out. Where was he going? If anyone on the farms saw him, they might come rushing up to interfere. He had to get away from all the farms and the shore, far away.

It has to be out over the dark depths, that's where this has to be decided, I must go far, far out—

And that was where he seemed to be rowing now.

I've never been here before, he began telling himself.

He glided along, out of place somehow, although everything around him should have been familiar.

Suddenly he raised his oars—and big drops of sweat appeared on his forehead. What was it? It was *here*. This was the place. He was hidden here and far from every shore, there was no longer any excuse. Just here! Mustn't think.

He shipped his oars. The water on them glistened in the sun. The boat glided along for a little while, then lay absolutely still.

'Well, Hege, the time has come,' he said across the surface of the lake.

He'd wanted to say this in a loud and firm tone, but didn't succeed. On the other hand he managed to carry out his plan without any bother. With numb fingers he removed the loose board and uncovered the weak spot. His foot felt numb as well, but he stamped hard on the rotten plank, and it went through at once. He jerked his foot back as if he'd been stung. The water came gushing in through the hole. He grabbed hold of the two huge oars and sat trembling in the bottom of the boat with one under each arm.

But where's my body? he thought. Who is it who's doing all these things? This isn't me. Now we'll see what's meant to happen.

The boat soon filled up. It was completely water-logged, and when the water reached the top it sank quietly beneath him. Before he realized what was happening, he was left floating on the oars. Just as he'd intended.

The water wasn't cold. It still retained some of the warmth of summer. But the black depths seemed to snatch at his feet, and Mattis gave a jerk. Only his head remained above the surface. He began kicking out, and swung his arms wildly in an effort to push himself towards the shore he was trying to reach. He was allowed to do that, that was part of the plan. He thrashed about like a madman, making an odd splashing noise, and he actually moved forward. The lake was like a mirror, sky and earth lay there upside-down.

Mattis pushed himself forwards, was staring fixedly at a point on the western slopes. The point nearest to him. He must plough his way through the water with every ounce of strength he could muster—that was part of the plan.

A puff of air moved across the lake after a while, as if someone had breathed on it. Here and there a shadow landed on the surface, but Mattis didn't notice. He struggled and gasped for air and went on pushing himself slowly forwards in the same direction. In the meantime a bank of cloud had risen over the horizon—he didn't see that either.

He didn't see anything any more, it was as much as he could manage to push his way forwards without falling off the oars. His body still felt strange and numb, and as heavy as lead too. The distance he had covered was as nothing compared with what was left. He was almost as far away from the shore now as when he had started.

'Hege!' he shouted all of a sudden—he had seen the wind coming. So the wind was coming after all! The gentle breath of air had quickly changed to wind. In the distance Mattis could see a dark-blue line stretching right across the surface of the water, and his face turned pale. It was quickly moving nearer. Blue and strong the wind sped from the clouds behind him—soon the lake would be in a turmoil.

Already the wind was whipping up white crests on the waves; they would soon fill Mattis's mouth with water and rob him of breath. Before long he would lose the oars.

'Mattis!' he shouted in his confusion and utter helplessness. Across the desolate water his cry sounded like the call of a strange bird. How big or small that bird was, you couldn't really tell.